SQUATCH OUT!

A BIGFOOT SHIFTER ROM-COM

DEYSI O'DONAL

Copyright © 2025 by Deysi O'Donal

All rights reserved.

No part of this book may be reproduced in any form or by any electronic or mechanical means, including AI training, information storage and retrieval systems, without written permission from the author, except for the use of brief quotations in a book review.

Any resemblance to actual places or people, either living or dead, is purely coincidental. Or used in a purely fictional manner.

No part of this book or any of the cover art has knowingly used generative AI. I support 100% human creativity.

cover by GetCovers

Edited by Mountains Wanted

Chapter Headers made with Canva Pro

 Formatted with Vellum

CONTENTS

Untitled	vii
Chapter 1	1
Chapter 2	13
Chapter 3	27
Chapter 4	37
Chapter 5	47
Chapter 6	53
Chapter 7	65
Chapter 8	73
Chapter 9	83
Chapter 10	89
Chapter 11	97
Chapter 12	103
Chapter 13	117
Chapter 14	123
Chapter 15	137
Chapter 16	151
Chapter 17	161
Chapter 18	171
Chapter 19	177
Chapter 20	185
Chapter 21	193
Chapter 22	203
Chapter 23	215
Chapter 24	225
Chapter 25	229
Chapter 26	237
Chapter 27	243
Chapter 28	249
Chapter 29	259
Chapter 30	269

Afterword	275
About the Author	277
Also by Deysi O'Donal	279
Also try Poppy Aster	281

For Anna.
Thank you for encouraging me to try something new.

SQUATCH OUT!

DEYSI O'DONAL

OLIVIA

CHAPTER ONE

My heart trips rapidly with anxiety as the plane's engines roar to life. Chaotic butterflies begin to swirl deep inside my stomach, and I squeeze my eyes shut when the sudden burst of speed pins me to my seat. Gripping the armrest with one hand, I press the other onto the back of the seat in front of me, holding my breath against the feeling of lightness when the plane leaves the runway and soars up into the early dawn sky.

The butterflies are rioting now with excitement. I'm really doing this! I've been planning this trip for almost a whole year. Saving up my PTO and working extra hours. I'm an HR recruiter, so I had to make sure my caseloads were taken care of and my clients and coworkers weren't left hanging. It was a lot of work, but I made it! Today is the day, and I'm finally flying out of Roanoke and heading across the country to meet up with friends for a week of camping in the Pacific Northwest wilderness. *Bigfoot country.*

When the plane reaches altitude and the seatbelt sign blinks off, I finally lean back into my seat and let myself relax. I'm not much of a traveler. In fact, the last time I traveled across the country, it was in the back seat of my parents' minivan. I was seven years old and packed up with the rest of our worldly possessions. I'm no less packed-in this time around—squished between a young woman who smells strongly of weed and an older man who doesn't look a day under one hundred and five.

Next time, I vow to myself, *I'm paying extra for an aisle seat.*

I'm just starting to relax, hoping to sleep through the five-ish hour flight when I feel a tap on my forearm.

"You got family in Seattle?" Weed Girl is grinning at me from her spot next to the window. She has an *earthy* vibe that goes along with her strong scent. "Or are you traveling for business?"

I look down at my favorite hoodie—featuring a blurry image of Bigfoot throwing up the peace sign and riding the Loch Ness monster under a hovering UFO—and wonder what part of my outfit made her think I might be traveling for business.

She's wearing a colorful Boho-style outfit, and her sandy-colored hair is pulled up into a messy bun. Beautiful designs cover the backs of her hands and long fingers that are either henna or tattoos. I bet she works in or owns a small boutique filled with crystals and local art.

"Um, neither actually," I say. "I'm just meeting friends."

"Oh yeah?" She turns in her seat, leaning back against the closed window, getting comfortable for what she must think will be an interesting conversation to pass the time. "What are you planning with your friends?"

My lips twitch because, if I know anything, it's how to shut down a conversation.

I imagine she assumes I mean taking in the party scene, or maybe a wedding or family reunion. I glance over at the elderly man on my other side, but he's fast asleep with his chin on his chest.

"Actually..." I try my best to fold my ankles under my seat and turn so my body is angled toward her. A wide grin spreads across my face. "We're going camping in the Olympic Mountains," I look around and then lean forward, dropping my voice like I'm about to tell her a secret, "to look for bigfoot."

Her smile falters, and her eyes grow wide. "B-bigfoot?"

"That's right." Settling back into my seat, I fold my arms across my chest and watch her rethink her decision to say hello to me.

"And you believe bigfoot exists?" She looks around for an escape. Of course, there is none, so now she's probably wishing she picked a different seat. Or kept her pleasantries to herself.

"I do." I nod, then I lean in again, letting her in on an even bigger secret. Not that this stranger is likely to believe a thing I'm about to tell her. "My friends and I, we've seen one."

"You... have?" Now she's looking around frantically.

"Uh-huh. With so many sightings all around the world, there must be thousands of them. Maybe even more. You know?"

"I–uh–had no idea..." Her eyes keep sliding away from me, trying to find a way out of the awkwardness I'm serving. But I just keep talking.

"I was six when I saw it. My family was visiting Mount St. Helens. Have you ever been there?"

She shakes her head, and I *tsk* at her. "You should visit; it's amazing. Anyway, I got distracted by the dappled sunlight filtering through the lichen-covered trees and ended up wandering away from my parents where I found myself all alone in a dense patch of forest."

All these years later, the memory is still as fresh in my mind as the day it happened.

When I realized I'd gotten myself lost, I started to cry. I knew, if you get lost, you're supposed to stay put so an adult can find you. But logic quickly took a back seat to my fear of possibly being eaten by a wild animal, and I started frantically trying to find my way back to my parents. Of course, that only got me even more lost.

The sun was starting to set when I collapsed in the middle of a small clearing. Wrapping my arms around my knees, I curled into a ball and sobbed. I don't know how long I sat there before I realized there was a strange sound repeating over and over, like it was trying to get my attention. It was a deep wuff. *Almost like a throat clearing.*

When I looked up, I saw a huge hairy figure peeking out at me from behind a tree. Blinking away my tears, I rubbed at my eyes, certain I was seeing things, but it was still there when my vision cleared. It made a wuff-wuff *sound and then disappeared around the tree.*

After jumping to my feet, I followed it.

I don't know how I knew that I should. The thought that it might hurt me never occurred to me until I was much older.

Every few dozen yards, it would appear around another tree and make the wuff-wuff *sound before disappearing again. It led me through the darkening forest until I heard the panicked sound of my mother's voice calling out my name.*

By then, I'd been missing for hours, and, of course, no one believed me when I told them about the giant monkey-man that led me back. After I was reunited with my parents, holding on to my mother's hand, I looked over my shoulder back into the forest. Looking back at me was the same hairy creature. A creature I would later realize was the legendary

Bigfoot and it sparked an obsession that has stuck with me all these years later.

When I finish telling her my story, she mumbles something like, *"That's fascinating,"* and grabs a pair of pink headphones so she can ignore me. Settling back in my uncomfortable seat, I tuck a neck pillow behind my head and close my eyes. My lips quirk up at the corners and no one bothers me for the rest of the flight.

FIVE HOURS LATER, I'm the first of my friends to land in Seattle.

While I make my way through the sprawling airport, I pull out my cell and text Tony.

We were teens when we met on a message board devoted to bigfoot. Both of us were young when we had our sightings, which kind of cemented our friendship. Over the years, we've stayed in touch, despite college and jobs and just life in general. Now he's one of my best friends and the closest thing to a brother I've ever had.

My parents had me when they were older. My mom was in her fifties, and my dad was sixty. I was *a pleasant surprise* after years of infertility, but it meant losing them before I graduated from college. My mom first, to cancer, and my dad less than a year later from his broken heart.

> ME: Just landed.

Almost immediately, I see the dots flashing under my message.

> TONY: So jealous! I'd give anything to stretch my legs right now. I still have two more hours till I land.

Tony is flying in from Colorado.

> ME: Be glad your flight isn't as long as mine was. I got stuck in the middle seat.

TONY: I told you to upgrade.

> ME: 😏 Yeah, well, I spent all my money on reserving our campsite. Speaking of spending money, I'm going to hit REI and Trader Joe's before I head up to the lodge. Drop me a list of anything else you can think of that we might have forgotten.

TONY: Don't worry about us. We'll pick up anything we need on our way. See you soon!

> ME: Can't wait!

Swiping my thumb across my phone screen, I open another text message. This one is for Brian.

> ME: Hey, Brian. Just landed. Let me know when you and Ashley land. I can't wait to meet up with everyone!

I wait a few minutes, but when I don't receive a reply, I tuck my phone away and keep moving toward the baggage claim. Apparently, it's conveniently located at the opposite end of the massive airport from where we landed.

I met Brian and Ashley on the same message boards I met Tony. Since they are both from Montana, they decided to fly together. I've known Brian for several years; he's probably old enough to be my father but acts like a man closer to my age. I haven't known Ashley for as long, but I'm excited to get some much-needed girl-time this week.

This will be my first time meeting them both in person,

and I can't help the excited spring in my step as I collect my luggage. It's not much; I have my carry-on with me, so I'm only picking up a large clamshell tote with my camping gear. That finished, I head off to find the car rental place.

I'M GRIPPING the steering wheel so hard, I'm surprised my fingers don't leave permanent impressions in the plastic as I finally merge onto the highway that will take me north toward the Olympic National Forest.

Fucking hell. I thought traffic in Roanoke was bad, but this place is so much worse!

Seattle drivers seem to have no concept of what a blinker is, and none of the road signs are helpful at all, leaving me at the mercy of my lagging GPS. Despite that, I managed to get the rest of the supplies I wasn't able to bring with me on the plane and some groceries without getting into a major traffic accident.

Glancing beside me, I let out a heavy sigh. When I booked my trip, I made sure to reserve a full-sized SUV, knowing I'd be hauling a lot of gear and driving in rough terrain. But when I got to the car rental place, the bored-as-fuck kid behind the counter informed me that all they had was this compact hatchback. When I raised a stink, I was told I could take it or leave it.

At least it has all-wheel drive. But I had to fold the back seats down and flatten the front passenger seat to fit my trunk inside. Hopefully the others chose a better rental place and will have better luck.

A giggle slips past my lips as I imagine the three of them pulling up in a compact sedan that would have trouble handling a gravel road, let alone the terrain I'm expecting. Not to mention how it would hold the three of them and all their gear.

The drive up Highway 101 is beautiful, and it's not long before my stress is melting away. It's a sunny day on the Washington coast, and I'm captivated by the blue sky and shimmering ocean. About an hour into the three-hour drive, I get a text from Tony announcing they have landed and will be hitting the road to meet me soon.

Another wave of excitement hits me. It has been far too long since I've taken a real vacation, and the mountains have always been my happy place. Back home, it's not uncommon to find me heading up into the Appalachians on my days off. Add some of my favorite people and the potential to maybe spot a bigfoot, and I'm the happiest nerd in the world.

The small town where we'll be staying tonight is the last bit of civilization before we'll head into the uninhabited and unforgiving Olympics. We booked rooms at a luxurious lakeside lodge for tonight and then another night when we return, since the campsite I reserved for the five-day stretch has an outhouse, and that's it. No running water. No shelter. Just earth and sky and hopefully a Sasquatch.

More giddy anxiousness hits me as I get closer and closer to my destination, and I dance a little in my seat. I chose the Olympics rather than the more popular forests to the south, where my own sighting took place, because of a run of recent sightings in the area. For months, I researched maps and trails before finally deciding which camp will give us the best chance of seeing an elusive bigfoot.

Being a bigfoot enthusiast can be lonely. Most people don't want to know that you believe in a magical, make-believe creature. Just like on the plane with Weed Girl, when the subject comes up, my story is nearly always met with skepticism at best and outright disgust at worst.

Smart career women are *not* supposed to believe in fairytales. Or bigfoot.

Which is fine. I'm not out to change anyone's mind. I know what I saw. Although, it would be nice to end up with some irrefutable proof that what I experienced as a child was real. To be able to prove there really is an entire species of ape-like cryptids wandering the forests and mountains all around the world.

The voice of C-3PO suddenly comes to life through my GPS, *"Did you hear that? Your destination is coming up on the right."*

I hit my blinker, preparing to turn off the highway when I notice a sign for Forks. You know, the home of a certain series based on sparkling vampires. Biting down on my bottom lip, I debate keeping straight so I can visit the town that's been made famous by my favorite books. Because, big surprise, the nerdy bigfoot girl is also Team Edward.

Knowing how close I'd be, one of the first things I did when I booked this trip was check the availability of Bella Swan's house that's been made into an Airbnb. Sadly, it was booked out for the entire month, but I'm definitely planning to make a trip to visit it before I have to fly back to Virginia.

With a heavy sigh, I take my exit.

A few minutes later, I'm passing a rustic wooden sign welcoming me to Seli Lake. There isn't much to the small town other than a general store, a couple bars, gas station, and some fast-food places. C-3PO leads me down the two-lane main street and then around a corner where the main attraction comes into view. The Seli Lake Lodge is the largest building in the whole town and sits on the shore of the lake that gives the town its name.

The missed opportunity to visit Forks is completely

forgotten as I pull into the parking lot. Lush green landscaping curls around to the back where the lake softly laps at the shore. The three-story lodge is shingled with cedar siding and trimmed with a coat of unblemished white paint. Behind me, the sinking sun reflects the red and orange sunset across all the west-facing windows.

"You have arrived!" I cut C-3PO off as I turn off the engine. Then I just sit for a minute, taking in the rustic, yet posh view.

Damn, this place is even nicer than the website claimed. Pushing open my door, I step out into the humid evening. As lovely as this is, *I can't wait to get up into the mountains.*

CHAPTER TWO

> TONY: Hey, Liv, we're HERE!

I'm sitting cross-legged on my plush bed, freshly showered, with my hair wrapped up in a towel that smells strongly of bleach. A huge grin stretches my cheeks as I type back.

> ME: Sweet! I'll be right down.

Nervous energy courses through my body as I give my hair a good scrub with the towel and then do a quick run-through with my fingers before jumping off the bed and heading out into the hall. When I get to the elevator, I remember I'm wearing plaid sleep pants and a t-shirt that announces, *I like boys who sparkle.*

Shit. My poor taste in pop culture t-shirts is not the first impression I planned to make, but I can't exactly stop the elevator and go back now. As soon as the doors open to the lobby, I spot Tony. His back is to me, but I'd know him anywhere. He's standing by a fireplace that's big enough I could probably stand inside it, if it wasn't lit and crackling cheerfully.

As if he can feel my eyes on him, he turns around, and a guilty look flickers across his face. It's there one moment and gone the next, replaced with his familiar wide grin.

He looks just like he always does, wearing his signature black track pants and a matching red and black pullover. He opens his arms wide, his teeth flashing white against the dark scruff that covers his jaw and cheeks, and darts across the lobby toward me.

I meet him halfway with a squeal when he lifts me off my feet to spin me around.

I'm still laughing when he finally sets me back on the ground. "What's this?" I ask, reaching up to pat the side of his cheek.

"My girlfriend says I look hot with a beard." Tony rubs at his cheek. I'm pretty sure he's blushing behind his neatly trimmed whiskers.

"I dunno." Stepping back, I cross my arms over my chest and narrow my eyes at him. He's not much taller than me, so I can mostly look him in the eye as I examine him. "I think you still look like a punk. How is Carmen? I was really hoping she would come with you so I could finally meet her."

His smile turns goofy, and my heart floats a little when I realize he is so in love with her. They've been dating for almost four years now, and I make a mental note to pester him about why he hasn't asked her to marry him yet.

Sometimes I wish I could find my person. Someone to share my life with. Who accepts and maybe even embraces my quirks. Someone I can feel the same toward.

"She was out the minute she learned there weren't five-star amenities." Tony laughs. "She sends her love though. I know she really wants to finally meet you too." His dark eyes dart to the side, and his smile falters. "Uh, Liv, there's something–"

Before he has a chance to finish, Brian strides up to us. My grin is still in place as I turn to him and freeze.

Brian looks exactly the way I'm expecting, having seen him online and talked to him through video chat. He's tall and dark-skinned with warm brown eyes and long, lean arms and legs. It's the person behind him who has me stumped because, instead of seeing Ashley coming to stand beside him, there is a strange man.

"Uh, who's this?" I glance between him and the tall blond man. He's definitely not the pink-haired woman I was expecting.

Completely unbothered by—not to mention, ignoring—my question, Brian holds his arms out to hug me. "Livie! I'm so glad to finally get to meet you in person!"

"Brian, where's Ashley?" I ask again, stepping back instead of leaning in to hug him back.

Brian's smile slips and turns forced. "I'm sorry, Livie. Ash had an emergency at the last minute and had to call off. There wasn't time to tell you." He turns and motions to the man beside him. "This is Darren. Since Ashley couldn't make it, I invited him."

I look over at Tony. He has the same guilty expression I noticed when I first saw him. "Did you know he was coming?"

Tony starts to shake his head, but then nods and admits quietly, "Not until he came off the plane with Brian."

I look back at Darren, who looks like a nice enough guy, but–

"Brian, why didn't you say something?"

"It was literally last night. There wasn't even time to cancel."

"But there was time to invite another person?" I take a deep breath to calm some of the panic building up in my chest, not loving the way this is turning out. "Look, being the only woman camping in the middle of nowhere with three men is not what I was planning. I'm sure Darren is great, but you really should have told me—*us*—before just taking it upon yourself to change plans like that."

"Awww, Livie, don't be like that," Brian whines.

I grind my molars at being called Livie for the third time, just as Tony steps up beside me. "Olivia is right; you should have said something instead of going behind our back. Inviting someone we don't know is a pretty dick move."

Brian hangs his head, and Darren steps forward, sticking his hand out to me, "I'm sorry. I didn't mean to cause any trouble. It's Olivia, right? I've seen you and Tony around the boards; it's nice to meet you."

He's handsome, and his smile is lopsided, which gives him a boyish look. He's dressed for comfort, in loose jeans and a t-shirt. His dirty-blond hair is in need of a trim, and bright blue eyes stare deeply into mine as he talks. It's slightly unnerving, but not inappropriate exactly. Still, I find myself giving his hand a quick shake before stepping back with a nervous smile.

"It's nice to meet you too." When he mentions the boards, I'm able to put his name with his online persona, and some of the stranger-danger eases up a little.

Darren's been around the boards longer than I have and moderates several chats. However, other than knowing him by name, I don't know much else about him, and I'm still pissed that Brian switched out Ashley for this guy without a heads-up.

I glance beside me at Tony, who gives me a sympathetic look that says, *I've got your back, whatever you decide.*

With a long sigh, I give Brian a warning look. "Well, we're already here now."

Brian brightens up and then claps a hand on Darren's shoulder, giving him a *see, I knew it would be fine* look that makes me want to change my mind.

"I don't know about you, but I'm dying for some real food," Brian announces as he takes in my casual outfit before stopping at my bare feet. "We are still planning to have dinner together, right? Or did you want to get room service?"

"Shoot!" I look down at what is basically my pajamas. "I totally forgot we were planning dinner together. After the long flight and drive, I couldn't wait to get comfortable. If you give me a minute, I can change."

"I need to drop this off in my room, too," Tony adds, giving his carry-on a spin. "Let's meet back here in ten."

WE HAVE dinner in the restaurant attached to the lodge. Tony, Brian and I mostly carry the conversation while Darren sits quietly, only speaking up when one of us asks him something directly. Mostly, it's a lot of the three of us catching up, since we've been friends online for so many years.

We start out by talking about what's been going on in our jobs and lives, but inevitably the conversation turns to the reason we are all here.

Bigfoot.

Or Sasquatch, if you like. Ape Man. Yeti. Menk. Skunk Man. Whatever you want to call it, to us they are merely variations of the same creatures.

"What would you do if you actually came face-to-face with one?" Brian asks around a bite of fettuccine.

Tony takes a moment to consider his question. "I dunno. Maybe try to get a picture of it. With my luck, my camera will break just as I try, though."

We all laugh, because Tony always runs into tech problems.

"I don't even care about getting proof or not," I respond as I dunk a thick French fry into the puddle of ketchup on the edge of my plate. "I just want to see one again, to reaffirm that I wasn't imagining it."

Brian and Tony nod their agreement, but Darren's expression flickers with confusion. As if the idea of not caring about proof is something he can't quite comprehend.

"I'll never forget my first sighting," Brian reminisces. Pushing his empty plate away, he leans back in his chair and jumps right into a retelling of the first bigfoot he saw as a long-haul trucker.

"It was the middle of the night, and I was just outside Missoula, coming back from South Dakota. There was a rest area coming up, and I was planning to stop there for the rest of the night, since my drive time was up. I was getting tired, but the second that hairy bastard stepped out of the trees and right into my headlights—well, that woke me the fuck up!" His dark eyes snap to me, and he quickly apologizes. "Pardon my language."

I shake my head and give him a wave, letting him know that it's fine, and I'm not bothered in the least.

"So, I'm standing on the brakes. My tires are squealing; the trailer is groaning like it's about to jackknife, and that motherfu—*er*—the bigfoot doesn't even glance my way. He just strides on by and disappears into the forest on the other side of the highway."

We laugh at his retelling, and then Brian turns expectantly to Tony. "Your turn."

"You guys know my story. I've told it a hundred times," he complains.

"Darren doesn't," Brian says, then leans back in his chair to hear it again.

"Fine," Tony says with a huff, but I know he loves telling it. We all do. "So, I was just a kid. I think I was twelve or something." He leans forward on his elbows and looks around the table at each of us. "My whole family was coming up the coast from Cali to Washington. One of my uncles died, so we were all coming for the funeral. We were somewhere along the Oregon coast, and we stopped at a little motel right off the highway for the night. It was a total shithole but, when you're a family of nine, that's what you can afford. And it was better than everyone trying to sleep in our cramped minivan.

"The motel was tucked up against the foothills of some heavily forested hills, and there wasn't much more than a gas station with a small market attached for miles in either direction. All of us were crammed into the single room. My parents got the full-size bed with the two babies, and the rest of us curled up on the floor."

Tony quirks the corners of his lips up then he drops his voice like he's telling a ghost story. "It's the middle of the night, and I'm jolted awake by the loudest, most god-awful sound you've ever heard. I lay there for a few minutes with my heart pounding, wondering if I was hearing things, when it came again. That time, it almost sounded like a baby screaming, so I panicked! What if it was one of my little brothers or sisters?

"Without thinking, I jumped up and ran outside. Our room was at the very far end of the motel, and except for a dim light above the door, everything was pitch-black. So I'm squinting, looking around, trying to see what might have caused that sound, when I hear it again. My head snaps to the side, and I see it." Tony's eyes are wide as saucers as he recalls what happened next.

"The bigfoot was right next to the motel, in the narrow space between the building and the forest. It had to be close to eight feet tall, and it was fighting with a full-grown cougar!"

"Wait. So, the sounds you heard weren't from the bigfoot?" Darren interrupts suddenly.

All eyes snap to Darren, then back to Tony, who shakes his head. "Nope. It was the cat making all the racket. The bigfoot never made a sound, at least, none that I heard. I was frozen stiff as I watched him wrestle with the cougar until he managed to grab it by the back of its neck with one hand, and just above the base of its tail with his other." Tony lifts his arms over his head in demonstration. "And then he *threw* that cat into the tree line."

We chuckle at the imagery. All of us except for Darren, who is still frowning at Tony, his expression shuttered with the same look non-believers often wear. Suddenly it occurs to me that I know nothing about *his* story. We all have one. No one ever just suddenly believes bigfoot exists. Sure, there are some who think *maybe* there's something out there, but only those who have seen it with their own eyes are the true believers. Darren's name is often bounced around the message boards with a kind of reverence, like he is some kind of all-knowing guru. But beyond that, I know nothing about this man.

After Tony finishes his story with how the bigfoot glanced over at him, lifted its large hand with a wave, and then followed the cougar into the trees, I turn my attention to Darren. "So, what's your story?" I break off a bite of buttery, perfectly cooked salmon with the edge of my fork. "What was it that made you believe?"

Any one of us might have smiled or maybe gotten a little shy at being put on the spot. Darren's blue eyes narrow and snap to me with a surprisingly hostile look before dropping to his barely touched NY steak. His jaw goes tight, and muscles flex in his joint from clenching his teeth.

He's quiet for a long time. Brian, Tony, and I glance across to each other curiously. Slowly, Darren picks up his knife and fork and cuts into his steak with more force than seems necessary. When he lifts his eyes to me again, his expression is eerily blank.

"One of them killed my brother right in front of me." He stabs his fork into one of the bites, shoves it into his mouth, and begins to chew angrily.

No one talks about bigfoot after that.

In fact, we hardly talk at all. We finish our dinner, and, in the awkward silence that follows, we each make our excuses that it's late or that we have to be up early the next morning. Tony and I leave together. Our rooms are a floor apart, while Brian and Darren's are on the other side of the sprawling complex.

I'm deep in my thoughts until we stop in front of the elevator. "Liv–?" Tony starts.

"Why didn't you tell me he was coming?" I cut him off. Tony's face crumples, and his shoulders hitch forward with his guilt. More softly, I add, "I wish you would have, instead of waiting to spring it on me."

"I'm really sorry." I can tell he means it. His face is tight with regret. "You're right, I should have given you a heads-up the second I met them at the airport, but we were already here and—" He shrugs.

I get it. Kinda. It's just that— "Something doesn't seem right with him." When I look up, Tony is nodding his agreement. "Do you know anything about Darren?"

"Not really." He shakes his head. "I know he has a reputation around the boards as being something of a bigfoot expert, but other than that and what he told us tonight—no, I don't know him at all."

One of them killed my brother right in front of me.

A chill runs through me as Darren's words repeat in my head. It's such a contradiction of mine and Tony's sightings, where the creatures acted on our behalf. One of them leading me back to my family and the other protecting Tony's family from a dangerous predator. Honestly, until this very moment, I never considered that they might be dangerous predators as well.

The elevator opens, and we step inside.

"Liv, do you want to call off this trip?" Tony asks as soon as we're closed inside the small space.

I stop for a second to think... *Do I?* My stomach is roiling with concern for the sudden uncertainty Darren has brought to our group.

"No..." I say slowly. Then, more firmly, "No. I don't want to do that." I wrinkle my nose, thinking of all the work I've put into this trip to just call it off. I look up at him. "Do you?"

"No," he sounds relieved, but then turns serious, "but after what he said at dinner... if he does anything that makes you uncomfortable, I want you to tell me and Brian."

I nod because that seems reasonable, although I really hope nothing like that will happen. Maybe this was just a one-off thing. Maybe he didn't really mean it the way it sounded. *Although he looked pretty damn serious when he said it.*

The elevator bounces to a stop, and the doors slide open on my floor. "I promise," I say as I step out into the hallway. "I'll see you in the morning."

Tony nods and then lifts his hand to wave as the doors slide closed between us. Shaking off the dour turn that dinner took, I turn down the quiet hall toward my room.

I hope I'm making the right choice by not canceling this trip. I'm still angry Brian took it upon himself to just invite someone without asking Tony or me, but I know Brian well enough that I can understand his reasoning for replacing Ashley when she had to cancel at the last moment. And I trust him and Tony—they'd never let anything happen to me.

After letting myself into my room, I change right back into the t-shirt and sleep pants I was wearing earlier. My mind is still tumbling over what Darren said at dinner as I wash my face and brush my teeth.

One of them killed my brother right in front of me.

Jesus, I will never unhear that. I don't know what was more chilling, his words or the absolutely deadpan way he said them. It's got me looking at this trip in a whole new light. Instead of being excited, now there is an apprehensive undercurrent. A few hours earlier, I couldn't wait to get up into the mountains. I was giddy at the prospect of seeing the creature that saved me when I was little. After Darren's story, I'm looking at it a lot differently now.

I'm reminded that all wild creatures have the potential to be extremely dangerous. Dangerous enough to kill someone, which isn't something I've considered before. Now I'm wondering what our plan would be in the event that we actually did run into one?

I turn off the lights and click on the TV to chase away the heavy transformation my thoughts have taken, scrolling until I find a rerun of *Friends*. Sliding between the cool sheets, I remind myself how excited I am to be here and to be heading up into the mountains in just a few hours. I hope I'll be able to sleep.

OLIVIA

CHAPTER THREE

The rising sun is still burning off the early morning mist as we get ready to hit the road.

With my venti quad shot oat milk latte in one hand, I press my back against the plastic trunk hanging out of the hatchback. Using all my strength, I push with my feet to get it to slide *just a little farther*. But it's not budging, and I'm regretting pulling it out so I could double-check my gear. *How the hell did I get it to slide into the car without any trouble yesterday?*

I can't help the way my eyes narrow with jealousy at the full-sized SUV the guys were able to rent from the same place, mere hours after I was told they didn't have the one *I* reserved.

"We've got plenty of room if you want to put that in our rig," Brian offers when he sees me struggling.

Muttering under my breath about *stupid misogynistic car rental companies,* I dig my heels in and give the trunk another push. This time it slides all the way in.

"Nope, I got it. Thank you, though." I turn around and slam the hatch shut with more force than necessary.

Tony joins Brian, followed by Darren a moment later,

and now all three of them are watching me with matching looks of confusion. Stifling the urge to flip them off, I remind myself they have no idea why I'm so irritated because I never mentioned the mix-up at the rental place. Instead, I go full passive aggressive and give them the most saccharine-sweet smile I can manage before stomping over to the driver side and slamming myself inside.

While I wait for them to finish loading up their stupidly roomy SUV, I sync my cell phone to the Bluetooth and queue up my playlist as I drink my caffeine overdose.

An eternity later, Brian backs out of his parking spot, and off we go. It's a two-hour drive to the remote campground I've reserved for the next five days, and now that we're on our way, my eagerness to get up into the mountains has returned.

The moment we turn off the highway and onto the two-lane twisty road that will take us to our destination, I realize that none of the pictures I saw online do this place any justice at all. With the sultry tones of Sleep Token blasting through the wimpy speakers, I stare in wonder at the unimaginably beautiful scenery. Rolling hills are broken up by dense patches of evergreens. Off in the distance, a large herd of elk graze, paying us no mind. Even farther off are the white-capped peaks of the Cascades, including one of the distinctive volcanoes that dot the range.

Most of the trip is up a steep and winding road, and I end up taking back every bad thing I ever said about my nimble little hatchback, since the larger SUV seems to be having much more trouble.

I bet it's using up twice as much gas too.

By the time we get to the small parking lot at the end of the road, the coffee has hit and I'm scrambling to get my seatbelt off and out of my car. I run right past the guys who have gathered around billboards with maps—and probably the rules of the park—heading straight into the rough-looking outhouse.

A few minutes later, feeling considerably lighter now that my eyeballs aren't floating, I join the guys at the maps.

Brian offers me a sympathetic smile before breaking some disappointing news. "The road that leads up to our campsite is more of a trail, and the site itself isn't going to allow two vehicles. So, you'll have to leave your car here and ride with us."

I wedge myself between him and Darren to squint up at the map. *Damnit, he's right*.

Honestly, I'm skeptical of *any* vehicles being allowed up the private trail. But it's getting late, and hauling all our gear on foot is definitely less appealing than riding with the guys and chancing breaking a rule.

Blowing out a sigh, I shrug. "It's fine." Then I head back to unload my car.

THE DRIVE UP to the campsite is...

It's breathtaking. I thought the drive through the mountains was beautiful, but this? It's... absolutely magical.

On either side of the dirt road that's not much more than a vague path, patches of late-season lupines and avalanche lilies dot the green rolling hills that rise to meet the jewel-blue sky before falling to kiss dense woodlands filled with evergreen and spruce.

The campsite is nestled along the aptly-named Windy Ridge, with lots of room for tents and a central firepit. Tucked several yards away inside a small shack, I spy the pit toilet. It's expectedly windy as I zip up my jacket over one of my favorite t-shirts that says, *I can do anything with a little sarcasm and profanity.* Then I jump in to help unload our gear.

We each have our own tent, and while I'm setting mine up, Tony starts a fire. By the time we're all settled, and our dinner is roasting on the grill, the sun has started to set. I lean back in my camp chair, a lightweight fleece blanket draped around my shoulders, as I watch the sinking sun set the sky on fire. While we eat, the thready clouds turn from vibrant orange with streaks of purple and magenta to royal blue before fading to a star-speckled black.

"When was the most recent sighting in this area?" Brian asks. He's on the opposite side of the fire from me and cast in shadow.

It's the first mention of bigfoot since dinner last night, and I don't like the way my chest tightens. But then I remind myself this is why we're here.

"There was a big one last summer." I pull out my cell phone. There is no service up here, but I saved some screenshots of the article I found. "A hiker was chased off the mountain."

The story had garnered a lot of attention when it hit the media, before it was quickly beat down. The witnesses were discredited, and it was called a hoax or misunderstanding before it faded away, like they all do. But it was the main reason why I chose the Olympics rather than the more popular forests in southern Washington and Oregon.

"Did it say anything else about what happened?" Tony leans forward expectantly.

"The article listed all the usual specifics," I reply. "The hiker was backpacking across the Olympics when he started noticing that sticks and pinecones were being thrown at him. Then there was the foul smell." I've always been curious why sightings are often preceded by a pungent scent. I don't recall noticing one when I was a little girl, but maybe I wasn't downwind? "When the hiker wasn't easily frightened off, the bigfoot charged at him from the trees. It was howling and making all kinds of noise as it chased the man back down the trail the way he'd come."

"That must have taken ten years off his life," Tony chuckles.

"Did the article mention what the howls sounded like?" Darren asks.

Brian turns to his friend. "Dude, you keep asking about noises. What gives?"

Darren presses his lips together, and for a minute, I don't think he will answer, but then he comes to a decision. "I have a theory, and I want to try something."

Before any of us can say anything, he's out of his chair and rifling through the back of the SUV. When he comes back, he's got his cell phone in one hand and a speaker in the other.

"I have a recording of a sasquatch mating call," Darren says, dead serious.

I've heard of hunters playing sounds they believe are from bigfoot, but their results have been mixed, and I've never heard of them producing any solid proof.

"How do you know it's a mating call?" Brian sounds skeptical, and the firelight that dances across his face makes him look like he's starting to question his decision to bring Darren along.

Darren stares down at his phone at the sound bite he has queued up. "I trust my source," is all he says.

Something about this has my stomach twisting with nerves. "I don't know—" I start to say, but he ignores me and flips on the speaker.

A low hum fills the night just before he pushes a button and the most *god-awful* screaming cuts through the silence.

It's so sudden, it startles me, and I slap my hands over my ears, but that's not enough to keep it out.

"Stop!" I shout.

But he's not listening. Instead, he's scanning the trees with a hopeful expression that smooths out the harsh lines he's worn since yesterday.

"Darren!" I yell as loud as I can, jumping up from my chair and stalking toward him. "Turn that off!"

The screams coming from the speaker send all the hair across my body standing on end and makes my stomach clench. Behind me, the other guys have also started yelling at him to turn it off.

He continues to ignore us, and I snatch the phone from his hand. My fingers fumble with the smooth surface but eventually I hit the stop button, plunging us back into a thick, blissful silence.

"*Jesus fucking Christ*! What is wrong with you?" I snap.

For a moment, his lip curls, and he looks like he's going to be mad, but then his eyes snap to the tree line behind me. The way his eyelids peel wide sends a rush of adrenaline flooding my system. My heart kicks rapidly in my chest, and I slowly turn around. My mouth falls open as a group of trees begin swaying frantically like something *big* is coming down the side of the ridge, knocking them aside in its wake.

No way.

I look over at Tony and mouth the words, "*Are you seeing this?*"

When he glances at me, his eyes are just as wide as Darren's, and he shakes his head with disbelief. My mind races to come up with a reasonable explanation for what could be knocking those trees around like that. Elk? Maybe if it's a whole herd. A moose? Bears?

I start backing away. Everything I've read says only

black bears live in these mountains, and they would be far too small to cause that much movement.

Just before whatever is coming toward us should have burst out of the tree line, everything suddenly stops. Seconds stretch, and when nothing else happens, we slowly relax.

"Can you believe that?" I giggle nervously.

Brian barks out a single harsh laugh, and Tony lets out a relieved breath. "For a second there, I really thought–"

A throaty growl echoes from the darkness, preceding a *huge hairy creature* that suddenly bursts through the trees, heading straight toward us.

Oh, shit—

For a moment, we're all frozen as we watch the creature's long arms swing angrily in time with his longer strides. *And that's not the only thing swinging.*

My mouth drops open at the sight of the baseball bat-sized erection bouncing back and forth across his thighs with each step.

I give my head a shake, managing to drag my gaze away from his raging boner to his face. Heavy brows are dropped low over sharp eyes. His wide mouth is turned down at the corners in a—*wait.*

My heart starts pounding anew because Bigfoot and his swinging dick are coming straight for *me*.

I start to backpedal, trying to keep my balance without tripping on the uneven ground as he barrels toward me. Darren stands frozen while Tony and Brian snap to action to come to my rescue.

"Hey!"

"No!"

They yell, coming at him from the side, but the bigfoot merely uses a giant hand to easily shove them aside, knocking them to the ground, before colliding with me.

Big hands circle my waist, and I scream as he lifts me off my feet like I weigh nothing. I fight against him with everything I have, pushing at him with my hands and kicking out with my feet to no avail. He tosses me over his shoulder without missing a stride and breaks wide when my protectors come at him again. He just barely avoids them before disappearing back into the trees the way he came.

CHAPTER FOUR

Twenty minutes earlier...

I fall back into my recliner with a groan.

After hiking up and down the mountain, all I want to do is kick my feet up and watch some mindless show for the rest of the night. With a steaming bowl of stir-fry in one hand and the TV remote in the other, I pop the footrest up as I scroll through the satellite channels to the latest episode of the cowboy series I've been watching.

My brother and I have worked for the forest service since we were practically kids. And as card-carrying members of the Coast Salish peoples, we're also kind of responsible for making sure the old treaties signed between the government and tribes are enforced. I've always taken that to mean we're something like caretakers for this stretch of the Olympic range.

It's already been a busy season, with warmer-than-usual weather, but the next couple weeks will be some of our busiest as tourists try to squeeze in their last-minute vacations before the kids have to go back to school. Trekking up and down the mountains is hard work, but as I'm getting older—I turned thirty-five just last month—I'm beginning to feel like something is missing. I don't enjoy the mountains as much as I used to. I'll always prefer the open spaces and nature to being stuck in the city, but lately I find myself getting...lonely up here all by myself.

Sure, I've got my brother for company, and the other rangers are as close as family, but that just means half the time we're at each other's throats. Not to mention, being this far from civilization makes it hard to find women. The ones who spark an interest usually aren't looking to settle down. I used to be more than fine with the no-strings hook-ups. But I'm starting to find myself wanting something *more*.

As the familiar score for the series starts to play, I dig my fork into the bowl of rice and veggies. The strong scent of ginger and soy sauce stings my nose, and my mouth waters in anticipation of the tangy-sweet flavor when suddenly, a loud scream cuts through the quiet night.

My hand pauses in front of my wide-open mouth.

What the hell is that?

The sound comes again, and the hair down the back of my neck stands up. It sounds like...*something roaring?* It's nothing like any of the usual animal sounds I'm used to, and it seems to be coming from somewhere down the mountain.

I mute the show and set my dinner aside as I rock forward, straining my ears as another growling screech cuts through the quiet.

What is that? My sensitive hearing picks out what could be a cougar's sharp yelp but with undertones from a grizzly bear's snarl. It's definitely not something natural, more like something that's been tampered with and... *digitized*? Whatever it is, it's got my curiosity triggered, and I kick the footrest out of my way.

The longer I listen, it becomes clear it's on a loop. Then realization hits me.

Shit, the god-awful howling is meant to sound like a *sasq'ets* in distress.

My brother and I share a very rare, *very secret*, genetic mutation. It's a gene that only a very small number of families throughout the world share and we're one of a handful of families along the West Coast. Few people know anything about it since most wouldn't believe us if we told them.

Owen and I are *sasq'ets*. More commonly known as *sasquatch*. Or simply squatch.

After pushing myself out of my chair, I'm out the door and heading down the mountain toward whoever is responsible for the recording. My mind is churning as I prepare myself for a confrontation with a group of bigfoot hunters. We get them on occasion, and after last year's "sighting," where my brother had to chase a hiker out of restricted tribal land, I'm growing more certain that's what I'm going to find.

The howls grow louder as I run down the side of the mountain, realizing they are coming from Windy Ridge, a popular campsite.

The "hunters" tend to be the most obnoxious campers. They have something to prove and come up with the strangest means to get the proof they are seeking. Like thinking they can lure us from the forest with the equivalent of a deer call.

More often, the *proof* they actually get is nothing, and we don't have to do anything. Occasionally, a group gets lucky, though. Like the hiker last year. Lucky for us, most people don't believe that sasquatch actually exist, so we're able to spin most stories away from the truth.

When the howling suddenly cuts off, I slow my strides

and come to a full stop just inside the tree line. Now that I know what the sound is, and where it's coming from, I should just leave them be. They are secluded enough out here that they aren't bothering anyone. Since Owen and I are the only *sasq'ets* up here, I'll just give him a heads-up to be careful around Windy Ridge and keep an eye on them to make sure they don't cause trouble for other campers.

I'm about to turn around and head back up the mountain when the wind shifts and I'm punched in the face by the sweetest aroma. It goes straight to my head, and I greedily drag in more of the heady scent until it's filling my senses with notes of soft female and wildflower honey.

This woman's scent is as unexpected as it is arousing, and suddenly my clothing is gone, ripped to shreds from the sudden transformation as I go from human to squatch. My cock extrudes from its protective sheath to swing ahead of me as I rush through the trees toward the campsite.

My mind screams for my squatch to *stop,* but I'm half drunk on her pheromones as I stride into the open. Four pairs of eyes turn to stare at me, but I hardly notice them because all my focus is on the small female backing away from me. I growl softly as I stalk toward her, caught up in my instincts rather than the rational side that spews warnings as I drag more of her potent fragrance over my sensitive olfactory senses.

I'm no longer in control of my body.

She is my entire focus as my powerful legs eat up the distance between us.

Two of the men she's with come at me, trying to protect her, but I bat them away as if they were insects. Weak. They fall away far too easily, unworthy of being anywhere near this woman.

With my cock jutting out in front of me, leaking precum from the tip like a faucet, I reach for her.

Her golden-brown eyes are wide as she stares at my straining erection. A small pink tongue moistens her lips, and her slender throat works when she swallows. She drags her eyes up to search my face. For an instant, I see a flash of curiosity before her fear takes over and she spins around to flee.

But I'm faster.

Her scream is soft and musical as my hands circle her tiny waist. I shush her to let her know I would never hurt her, but she fights me. Fists and feet land harmless blows against my legs and chest as I lift her up and toss her over my shoulder. That nagging voice in my head is begging me to put her down, but the way her scent fills my nose with every breath has me under a spell as I turn back to the forest.

The two men have regrouped and come at me again, trying to take their woman back, but she's *mine*. I easily sidestep them, but they follow. My strides are much longer, and my powerful body is built for these woods, which makes it easy to leave them behind once I reach the trees.

My feet eat up the steep mountain terrain as the woman over my shoulder continues to scream and fight. Hiking her up higher on my shoulder, I offer more soft sounds, hoping to calm her. When that doesn't work, I clap a large hand over her ample denim-covered backside, groaning at how the stretchy material hugs her curves. Her sweet scent is even more potent this close to my nose, and it muddles the rational thoughts trying to break through my thick head.

"Hey!" she squeaks, beating on my back and twisting around on my shoulder. "Get your hands off me!"

I give her round bottom another squeeze and growl a warning for her to be still, enjoying the way her soft cheek feels under my palm. A shudder runs through me, and my cock pulses, dripping more pre-cum onto my thighs.

I've left the campsite far behind us when the nagging voice in the back of my mind starts up again.

What are you doing? Do you have any idea how many laws you just broke? Not just tribal laws, either. Kidnapping is a felony!

I pause. I've never felt this splintered before, like there are two separate beings in my body. I've always been Sean—whether I'm human or squatch. But suddenly I have this whole other instinct that has taken control.

I should take this woman to my cabin and apologize, then take her back to her campsite. But that idea, the very thought of letting her go, has my squatch snarling, and since he's currently in control, he climbs higher up into the mountains.

We need to take her somewhere quiet. Somewhere we won't be interrupted.

There is a cave not far from here, one of many throughout the mountain range. Owen and I call them *bugout caves,* since they're used as emergency shelters for anyone who finds themselves lost or trapped by bad weather. They are marked on most trail maps but are remote enough that I've only heard of a few humans ever using them. Mostly they are used by fellow Salish mountaineers and other squatch.

The higher I climb, the colder the air grows, until the woman over my shoulder falls quiet and begins to shiver. I pull her down, so she's pressed to my chest and shelter her with my furry arms.

Almost there, little one. I want to tell her, but speech isn't really a thing we can do as squatch. So, I pick up my pace instead.

By the time I reach the cave, her scent has completely gone to my head, and my cock is hard enough, I could pound nails with it. My fingers dig into her soft ass as I rip open the covering that's pulled across the cave's entrance. The air inside is stale and cold as I stride to the back where there is a small lantern.

My vision is far better in my squatch form, but even I can't see well in complete darkness, so it takes some fumbling with the light, hoping the cool temps haven't drained the battery. I let out a relieved sigh when it flickers to life.

With the small space illuminated, I tell myself that sliding her down the front of my body is completely unintentional and not at all so that I can feel her soft curves pressing against me once more.

The moment her feet hit the dirt-packed floor, she stumbles away from me, putting several feet between us. The corners of my lips quirk when I realize her sweatshirt has a picture of Bigfoot, Nessie, and a UFO. How appropriate.

She's breathing fast, and her plump pink lips are slightly parted as she stares down at my feet. Then, slowly, she drags her eyes up my legs before stopping at my hips where they widen at the sight of my cock pointing straight at her. She lets out a soft gasp and I wrap my fist around my thick length, letting out a deep groan as I squeeze.

I try not to imagine how much better her smaller hand would feel on my heated flesh, as I slowly glide my palm up my shaft to the glistening tip. Her eyes are locked on my hand as she staggers back and into the shelves that run along the back of the cave.

The bitter underlying scent of her fear flares between us when she looks past me to the opening of the cave. I can see her calculating the distance and how she might get past me, but then her eyes drop back to where my hand runs up and down my turgid length, and the sweet scent of her arousal takes over to fill the small space.

I keep stroking myself as I wonder if her hair, which is

the color of wheat in sunshine, is just as soft and silky as it looks. I step closer, wanting to test that theory, but my human side manages to push forward, and forces me to back up. My squatch snarls but accepts the small distance, making sure to keep myself between her and freedom.

What is happening? What am I doing?

Fuck, this is so wrong. I've never had my instinct ride me hard like this, to the point that I have lost all control.

Especially when the woman's eyes lock onto my pumping fist and her tongue darts out to slowly slide across her bottom lip. Her cheeks are pink, and her pupils are dilated, so that only a slight ring of her warm brown irises is visible. Her scent shifts, changing from wildflower honey to sweet sun-ripened peaches covered in thick cream.

Another low growl rolls from deep within my chest as I imagine her dropping to her knees before me. Parting those puffy pink lips then sticking her tongue out, looking up at me as she silently asks me to feed her.

Her eyes flare when I grunt, reaching my other hand under my pumping fist to grip my heavy sack, squeezing hard enough that my knees try to buckle, and my eyes slide closed. Behind my eyelids, I envision this pretty little woman closing her plump lips around the mushroom-shaped head of my cock. Swiping my thumb across the sensitive tip, I pretend it's her tongue, licking away the drops of pre-cum that collect there.

My testicles tighten as heat sears a path up my length. Pinching my fingers under the flared tip, I try to hold back my orgasm, but it's too late. My eyes fly open, and I focus on the woman across from me as the first lash of cum shoots across the packed-dirt floor.

Her mouth falls open in shock as I let out a deep groan and stroke out another spurt. A shudder racks my body, and I level my gaze on her when I ejaculate a third time. Letting out a hoarse bark, I milk my shaft with my fist as the last trickles of my seed spills over my fingers.

When I finish, I'm breathing hard.

The woman is staring at me. The expression on her face is hard to read. I'm expecting horror, but it's not that. It's not quite shock, either. It almost looks like—*excitement*.

But that can't be right.

Fuck. How many laws have I broken now?

Oh, no, you didn't just break them. You annihilated them.

Stumbling back a step, my blood turns cold with my embarrassment at what I've just done. I shake my head at her, trying to offer a silent apology before turning to run out of the cave and into the night.

OLIVIA

CHAPTER FIVE

With my heart pounding and my panties *drenched,* I lock my gaze on the dark entrance to the cave that ... that the bigfoot just ran out of.

Did—did that just really happen?

I glance down at the ground where the proof that he jacked off in front of me is splattered across the dirt floor.

No one is ever going to believe this.

In fact, if this ever gets out, I'm going to end up as an internet meme.

The minutes stretch, and when it doesn't look like he's going to come barging back into the cave, I slowly make my way to the entrance where a thick camouflage tarp is pulled back, letting in the harsh wind. It's pitch-black outside. There isn't even a sliver of the moon visible, and the dim light from the lantern behind me makes it seem even darker.

Leaning out of the entrance, I look down at the narrow ledge that disappears into the darkness. Finding my way off the mountain at night is off the table, unless I want to take the express way down. With trembling hands, I pull the tarp closed, securing it so the wind—*and hopefully the bigfoot*—won't blow it open again.

With the wind dampened, the small space begins to warm a little, but it's still barely above freezing, and all I'm wearing is my hoodie and jeans. The blanket I had around my shoulders is probably still in my camp chair.

I fold my arms across my chest to ease some of my shivering, unsure if it's from the cold or if it's shock that's setting in. My thoughts are a jumbled mess. I can't stop thinking about how Bigfoot looked as he stroked himself in front of me. I should feel horrified. *Disgusted*.

Instead, a shiver runs across my skin, and my breath hitches when I recall his intense eye contact that sent a rush of liquid heat soaking into my panties just before he came. Shaking those thoughts away, I kick some loose dirt over the mess he left.

Maybe hiding the evidence will make it easier to forget it happened.

Forcing my thoughts from Bigfoot, I take in the small cave he brought me to. It's set up like it's prepared for guests and not at all like how I would imagine a bigfoot lair would look. There is a human-sized camp bed against the far wall. Next to that is the row of shelves I was pressed against, with an assortment of necessities. *Human necessities.* Matches, a lighter, a first aid kit, tools and a flashlight. Then there are baskets filled with canned and nonperishable food and bottled water. On the other side of the cave, tucked into the opposite corner, is a small camp stove. The chimney is secured to the ceiling, and it disappears into a hole that must lead outside.

Rubbing my hands together, I drop to my knees before the small stove. The glass door opens easily, and the inside has been cleaned out so it's ready for the small pile of wood and kindling neatly stacked beside it.

I've just gotten a small fire going, when a loud snapping sound has me spinning around to where the tarp flutters wildly in the wind. I'm expecting an angry bigfoot, but when nothing comes crashing through the entrance, I let out a relieved sigh and make my way over to the camp bed. Tucked under it is a plastic container with bedding that has been vacuum-sealed. I force myself to focus on making up the bed, rather than the fact I was captured by a monster and brought up into the mountains.

When I've set up a cozy place to sleep, I tiptoe over to the tarp and peek outside once more. There is still no sign of the bigfoot, or anything else in the darkness. But I can't shake the worry that he'll come back.

Making sure the tarp is secured across the caves opening, I turn back to the shelves, I search through every bin for something I can use as a weapon in case I need to defend myself. I suppose it's too much to hope for a gun, not that I know the first thing about shooting one, but I do find a hunting knife with a blade as long as my hand. *That'll do.*

The adrenaline I've been running on is long gone, replaced by a bone-weary exhaustion. I add more wood to the stove and toe off my shoes so I can slide into the still freezing bedding. Clenching my teeth together to keep them from chattering, I tuck the knife under my pillow and then reach over and turn off the lantern. The flickering flames through the glass door are bright enough to chase away the oppressive darkness as I tuck the blankets under my chin and burrow in for the night.

After a few minutes, my cocoon finally starts to warm up, and soon I'm actually quite comfortable. Except that I'm trapped in a cave, on a mountain, with a monster outside somewhere.

With nothing else to do but let my mind spin wildly in the darkness, all the fear I've been holding back pushes to the front of my mind.

What if he comes back?

What if something else tries to break in?

Reaching under the pillow, I wrap my fingers around the knife, which makes me feel a little better. I wish I hadn't left my cell phone inside my tent. There's no reception up here, but at least I could play some games to distract me.

The guys must be frantic!

I hope they are okay. I saw how the bigfoot knocked them away when they came to my rescue. Tony especially looked like he took a pretty hard hit. Have they reported me missing? I wonder what kind of story they would tell the park rangers. I let out a sad little giggle, imagining them trying to convince them that a bigfoot stole their friend.

Hopefully someone will come to my rescue in the morning. I latch on to that, instead of worrying about being attacked in my sleep, but I still toss and turn while my mind races and overanalyzes everything that happened, like what I should have done, and what I need to do next. It must be close to morning when my lids finally grow heavy enough to stay shut and I slip into an exhausted, fitful sleep.

CHAPTER SIX

The walk down the mountain calms me enough that I'm able to shift back by the time I reach my brother's cabin. The windows are all dark, and I briefly wonder what time it is as I burst through his front door.

"Owen!" I shout, flipping on the living room lights. "We've got a problem."

My older brother is already standing in the doorway of his bedroom, wearing nothing but a pair of black boxer briefs and holding his sat phone against his ear. His eyes are squinty with sleep and his dark hair, streaked with silver, is sticking out all over his head. Whoever he's on the phone with must have woken him up just before I got there.

"What in the hell is going on—" he barks into the phone just as his head snaps up to look at me. "*Oh, fucking hell,* Sean!" Owen squeezes his eyes shut. "Dude, why are you naked?" He pinches the bridge of his nose and grumbles into the phone, "Hey, I'm gonna have to call you back. Sean just got here."

From across the room, I can hear the frantic voice on the other end.

Owen lets out a heavy sigh. "Yeah. Yeah. *I know!* Look,

tell the campers we're on it and that we'll touch base with them to let them know what we find." He glares at me, and I realize the call must be about the woman. "Uh-huh. Look, the longer you bitch at me, the longer it will take me to get out there. Okay. I'll keep you updated."

He pushes the end button with much more force than necessary and then drags in a deep breath, holding it before letting it out slowly. "What the fuck did you do?"

Crossing the room, I sit my ass on the edge of his couch and drop my head into my hands, trying to think of a way to tell him without making it sound worse than it already is.

There's really no sugar coating this, so I might as well tell him the truth and get it over with. I brace my elbows on my knees and look up at my brother. "I, uh, squatched out and sort of kidnapped a camper."

Owen doesn't blink as my words slowly sink in. Then he squeezes his fingers around the sat phone so hard, I'm surprised it doesn't crumble to pieces in his palm. I lean back when he pulls his arm back like he's going to throw a punch at me, only to stop at the last second.

"I know I'm going to regret asking, but *why*?" He drops into the chair across from me.

"Uh—" I have no idea why I did it. In fact, in hindsight, everything is kind of foggy.

Owen rubs his eyes with his free hand. He's probably using those calming breathing exercises he likes, to keep himself from murdering me.

"Okay," he says when he's no longer trembling with rage. "Tell me everything."

After taking a deep breath, I do, starting with the recorded howls that brought me down the mountain and then the unbelievably amazing scent that sent me squatching out and barreling out of the forest toward the pretty blond. I left out the part where I jacked off in front of her but explained that I left her in the bug-out cave not far from here.

"So, she's unharmed?"

My head snaps up, and I glare at him. "What? Of course she's unharmed!" I'm offended he would even think otherwise. He knows that I'd never hurt anyone, especially not a woman. We're no different as a squatch as we are as men.

Owen's shoulders droop with relief. When he finally looks up at me, his face is lined with disappointment. "You exposed yourself to four people, Sean. How the *fuck* am I supposed to fix that?"

My stomach clenches as the ramifications of what happened really hit. As hard as we try to keep our secret, it's getting harder and harder with technology. Camaras are everywhere, and me barreling out of the forest and through a campsite was not my best decision. Humans are *not* ready to learn that shifters exist.

"One of those guys is asking *a lot* of questions," Owen goes on. "I have a feeling he's going to cause us trouble."

He's scolding me like a stupid teenager, not that I can blame him. This is the worst kind of mess I could have gotten into.

Without a look at me, he punches a number into the sat phone and lifts it to his ear. "Hey, Ben? Sorry about earlier; I have good news. Sean found the camper up in the mountains. Since it was dark, he took her to one of the bug-out caves for the night. She'll be perfectly fine until morning."

He listens for a minute and then pinches the bridge of his nose again. "Uh, they said it looked like a *what*–?" He glares at me through his thick lashes, and I can't help cringing at what's going to come next. "I don't know what grabbed her. I mean, I guess it could've been a bear, but

Sean didn't say anything about her being injured, just shaken up."

By the time he hangs up with Ben again, Owen is clenching his jaw hard enough that I'm surprised his teeth don't crack. There is murder in his eyes.

"Fucking hell, Sean. You squatched out in front of a group of bigfoot hunters! Of all the—" He clenches his fists and takes some more deep breaths to calm down before he squatches out himself and throws me off the mountain.

A completely inappropriate laugh bursts from my lips. Owen has every right to be turned inside out over this. Being caught as a squatch is serious enough, but storming through a camp full of humans who are actively looking for us is...

Another laugh slips out, and I try to stifle it with my hand.

This is bad. Like, *really bad*.

But I can't stop laughing. When Owen gives me an unamused look, I just laugh harder.

Eventually, he gets up and leaves the room, and I'm able to settle down while the seriousness of this situation really sinks in. Cryptids like *sasq'ets* are kept secret for a reason. If humans knew we existed—hell, if they knew half of what we could do—they would hunt us to extinction. Either because they want to study us, hunt us for sport, or any number of other reasons that would drive them to wipe us out.

Owen returns a few minutes later, fully dressed and holding a bundle of clothes for me. The zipper on the jeans hits me across my cheek when he throws them at me, and my eye waters, but I say nothing. I suppose I deserve more than that for what I've done.

Luckily, we're close enough in size to share clothes. The extra pair of boots he drops in front of me are another matter. I've always had bigger feet, so I already know I'm going to be aching more than usual after the hike we're about to go on.

After I've dressed, he reappears, this time from the kitchen, with two travel mugs filled with coffee. "We'll check on the campers first, then we'll head up to the cave. By the time we get there, the sun should be starting to rise."

DESPITE THE LATE HOUR, the campers are still awake and sitting around their fire when we make it to their camp. I hang back as Owen talks to them, keeping my head down as I listen to him assure them that their friend—her name is Olivia—is safe.

I roll her name over in my mind, liking the sound of it there. My eyes slide closed at the memory of her pressed against my chest and shoulder. The way her syrupy-sweet scent filled my head and—

"Why didn't you just bring her back down with you?" My eyes snap open to find an angry bearded man standing in front of me. His fists are clenched at his sides, and he's trembling with rage.

I look over at where Owen is watching but not intervening.

I wonder who this guy is to her. A boyfriend? My nostrils flare when I scent him. I didn't catch his scent on her when I was carrying her over my shoulder, and he isn't carrying her scent now. A relative? No, there is no familial scent and no resemblance. Just a friend, I decide. Except, the thought that there might be more, or that there was ever anything more between them has me grinding my molars.

Something like jealousy bristles under my skin, and I remind myself that I should not have, nor do I want, any claim on this woman. My god, imagine the mess dating a bigfoot enthusiast would cause throughout the *sasq'ets* community.

Unclenching my jaw, I say, "It's too dangerous in the dark."

The man folds his arms across his chest and narrows dark eyes at me. Clearly not buying my explanation. "What were you doing up there that you were able to find her, anyway?"

The lie comes easier than I expect. "I was heading home from patrolling and heard screaming. When I got to her, she was alone. Frightened, but unharmed. That part of the mountain is rugged, and it wouldn't have been safe to bring her down, so I took her to a cave that was closer and easier to get to."

The man still looks skeptical, so I decide to try appealing to him: "Look. I've lived here most of my life, and I know these mountains better than anyone. The cave she's in has five-star accommodations compared to your tents. She'll be fine for the night. There are warm blankets, a wood stove, and food if she's hungry."

As Olivia's friend sizes me up, I can't help doing the same. I'm well over a head taller than him, but he's stocky, with a thicker build. Still, he wouldn't have a chance against me thanks to my preternatural strength.

"And she's alright? She wasn't hurt?" he asks, letting go of some of his bravado.

I nod, trying to reassure him as another man steps up beside him. This guy is lean and lanky, and he gives me a curt nod before dropping a hand on the shorter man's shoulder.

"See? She's alright, Tony," he says quietly. Then he

holds his hand out to me. "I'm Brian. We're not trying to give you trouble; we're just worried about our girl."

I swallow down a growl when he calls her *our girl,* just as Owen steps up beside me. "We'll bring her back down as soon as it's light," my brother promises them.

Both men nod, and my gaze wanders behind them, to the third man who is still standing by the fire. He isn't paying attention to any of this, nor does he seem to be at all concerned that Olivia is missing. Instead, his attention is focused on the trees.

"Darren," Brian calls out, and the man by the fire snaps his attention back to us. Brian has to wave him over, and even then, he hesitates before turning away from the forest.

"This is Darren. He played the recording that brought the—*the thing* out of the forest that grabbed Olivia."

The recording. I've been so focused on the woman, I forgot all about the strange howls that started this whole thing. "So. Tell me what happened here tonight," I ask the tall blond man who was so reluctant to join us.

"You already talked with Olivia. Didn't she tell you?" he snaps, looking like he'd rather be anywhere else.

"She did," I lie cautiously, "but we like to get all viewpoints during an investigation. If we've got a bear out here attacking campers, we—"

"It wasn't a bear," Darren cuts me off. His blue eyes gleam with anger, cutting through the darkness.

"Excuse me?" I force my voice to sound like I'm surprised, but in my mind, I'm rolling my eyes and thinking *great.*

There is something about his guy that isn't sitting well with me. He knows more than he should, in a dangerous way.

"I said it wasn't a bear," Darren repeats.

"Then what was it?" I have to work to keep my expression mild.

"It was a sasquatch." He says it matter-of-factly. Most people would be embarrassed to admit that was what they *thought* they saw. Not this dude.

"Look, sir." I carefully school my expression to look dismissive. It's my *let's humor the campers* look, and I've had years to perfect it. "There is no such thing as—"

"That thing that came out of the trees was no bear. It walked upright, just like a man, with his dick swinging, before he grabbed Olivia and ran off with her. You call that whatever you want, but it wasn't a bear."

I can feel Owen's eyes boring into the back of my head at Darrens mention of my dick, and I know I'll get an earful later.

Stepping back, I give Darren a nod. "We'll be sure to be on the lookout for a horny squatch, then." The heat of Owen's glare turns to laser beams at my snarky comeback.

"Is that all?" Darren grumbles. I don't miss the way his eyes keep darting into the trees, like he's expecting the squatch to come storming back through them at any moment.

"Actually, I'd like to ask you more about the recording." Owen steps up to him and drops his voice.

The blond man narrows icy blue eyes. "I don't know what you're talking about."

"Don't," I warn him. "We already know about it. I'd like to get your side of the story."

Darren's lips are pinched as he looks over at me and then at the other two men.

"He said it was a bigfoot mating call," Tony speaks up, and I don't miss the nasty look Darren shoots at him.

"And where did you get that?" Owen steps closer so he's crowding him with his much larger frame.

Darren's nostrils flare under his blade-thin nose, but he stays silent.

It becomes obvious he won't be giving us any useful information, not that it matters since the recording is nothing but noise anyway. It would be nice to be able to put some pressure on whoever might be spreading this ridiculousness.

Owen turns to Tony and hands him a business card from his wallet. "If you need anything, or think of anything that might be helpful, reach out."

Tony takes the card with a nod, and I don't miss his wary glance at Darren.

Owen and I exchange looks and head back to his truck.

"You're sure the recording wasn't legit?" he asks me as he turns the engine over.

"Yeah. It's probably something like a lion or maybe a bunch of different animals that have been meshed together and auto-tuned."

"Thank god," Owen sighs. "Although, I'm a little curious what a bigfoot mating call might actually sound like."

I bark out a laugh. So my big brother has a sense of humor after all.

The hike up to the cave is much slower in our human bodies, which gives us plenty of time to talk.

"What do you think about the Darren guy?" I ask.

Owen is quiet for a long time as he thinks. No one will ever accuse my older brother of being rash in a situation.

"He knows more than he should," he finally says. "I'm not sure how much of what he knows is accurate, though."

We keep heading up the mountain, letting the silence surround us. The sun is just starting to lighten the horizon when Owen suddenly looks over at me. "So why did you come barreling out of the forest with a hard-on?"

Heat floods my cheeks, but before I can think of an explanation, because I'm still wondering how any of that happened myself, the wind shifts. As if I called it to me, I'm hit with Olivia's honey and wildflower scent. It's like a slap to my face, and my skin starts crawling, signaling my shift. Only, I haven't called it.

When I don't answer him, Owen glances back at me just as my steps falter. "Are you alright?"

I open my mouth to growl at him that *I'm fine*, when another burst of wind brings more of her sweet scent. Ripe peaches and thick cream. My mouth waters, and my heart starts to race. Without any other warning, I squatch out, leaving Owen's clothes in shreds around me.

"Dude! What the fuck?" Owen jumps back from me, his eyes going to the pile of ruined clothing he let me borrow.

I'm not sure how this happened. I can't think of a time when I've ever shifted unexpectedly like this. Even when I was a kid learning how to control my squatch, he never just rushed forward like this. I usually had to coax him. And now it's happened twice without being called.

I whine my apology.

"Alright, just... just go home. Get your shit together, and I'll stop by your place after I bring the woman down the mountain."

With a low growl, I let him know I am not a fan of being ordered away like an unruly cub... but also, I obviously can't let Olivia see me like this. *Again*.

"I don't understand what the hell is going on with you, but let me handle this, okay? You go get some rest or something."

Hanging my head with a defeated huff, I turn around and start dragging my large feet back down the way we just came, being careful not to leave prints.

Olivia's sweet scent follows me, and I pause to look back up the ridge where Owen is making short work of the steep angle. He just turned forty, which might be considered midlife for a human, but you'd never know watching him.

I twist my neck, letting out a loud crack that radiates down my back, before turning back to trudge down the ridge. He's five years older than me, so why is it that suddenly I feel like I'm ready for retirement?

When I glance back up the ridge again, he's disappeared.

Letting out a heavy sigh, I continue making my way back down the mountain.

OLIVIA

CHAPTER SEVEN

The cheerful sound of whistling drags me from my deep sleep. I try to burrow deeper into the warm comfort of my blankets, but the sound keeps growing louder as whoever is whistling comes closer. I start to recognize the tune.

Oh, it's... it's... *wait*.

Who whistles to "Iris" by The Goo Goo Dolls? Whistles are reserved for old-timey songs like "She'll Be Comin' Round the Mountain" or something.

I'm blinking away the sleepy fog when the whistling abruptly cuts off, and whoever is out there clears their throat. "Um, Olivia? Are you awake?" a man's deep voice calls from the other side of the tarp.

Suddenly, the night before comes rushing back to me, and I'm wide awake. Bolting upright, I pull the blankets up to my chin with one hand and the knife out from under the pillow with the other. The cave is cold enough that my breath fogs the air, which means the fire must have burned itself out sometime during the night.

"Olivia?" the man calls out again.

"Yes?" my voice comes out high-pitched, and I clear my

throat before dropping it back to a normal tone. "I mean, yes. I'm awake."

"My name's Owen, and I'm a ranger. I'm here to help you back to your campsite. May I come in?"

Relief rushes out of me along with my exhale. "Yes, thank you."

The tarp flutters, and a hand pops through, holding an official-looking badge. "See? I'm not here to cause you any trouble, just to help," he insists.

"It's fine; you can come in." I can't keep back the soft laugh as I push the blankets aside, then think better of it and wrap a wool blanket around my shoulders when I'm hit with frigid mountain air. After swinging my legs over the side of the bed, I push them into my hiking boots to keep from freezing my toes on the cold ground.

The hand with the badge disappears, and then the tarp pulls back, just enough to let someone through. A very tall someone. Owen is broad as well as tall, and also lean enough to easily slip through the small space he made in the curtain. As soon as he's through, he flashes a disarming grin at me.

"Hi there," he says as he stands awkwardly by the cave entrance.

"Boy, am I relieved to see you!" I say with my whole heart, just before I notice he's handsome too. Like, *really handsome*. His skin is a dark tan, and his face is angular with chiseled cheekbones and full lips. His dark hair is cut short and shot through with silver strands. Deep lines are carved around the corners of his eyes, suggesting that he smiles a lot. He's wearing a thick red and black flannel jacket on top of a lighter-weight orange and green flannel shirt that clashes badly. As if he got dressed in a hurry or maybe he's color blind. His long legs are wrapped in denim, and heavy work boots cover his feet.

"I'm Owen Ferrell. Like I said, I'm a ranger. Your friends were worried when you... ah... were carried off."

He seems embarrassed, which means the guys must have told him exactly what it was that carried me off. I want to drop my face into my palms with secondhand embarrassment, because *of course* he wouldn't believe a word of it.

"I'm sure they are. It was pretty... sudden," I admit.

He gives me a stern side glance. "Are you hurt at all? Anything I need to know about? You have to be careful out here. The bears might look cute, but they are dangerous, especially the closer it gets to their hibernation."

"Bears?" Clearly I'm not caffeinated enough to follow what he's trying to say. But then it hits me, and I realize he's suggesting a bear carried me into the mountains. "Oh, right. *Bears.* And I'm fine; it—" *wasn't a bear,* "—it was dark, so..."

Owen turns, giving me a curious look. Like he knows I'm bullshitting him by going along with his story. "The mind can play tricks when it's dark," he mutters in response.

While I try to unpack his strange behavior, he looks around the small cave, and my heart does an embarrassed little flip when he glances down at the ground where the bigfoot shot his load. I covered it up. There can't be any way he'd know... right?

"Do you need anything before we get going?" he asks, turning his attention back to me.

Pushing the blanket off my shoulders, I shiver at the rush of cold air that hits me as I start folding the bedding that I slept in. "Just let me tidy up, and then—"

"There's no need. I'll send someone up to reset the camp, so it'll be ready if it's needed again." His mouth quirks, trying to hide his smile when he sees my bigfoot hoodie, and then his dark brown eyes flit over to the shelves filled with snacks. "Help yourself to anything you want for the way back down. We keep these caves stocked for hikers who might get stuck out here after dark, or in bad weather. And we check them regularly so everything is fresh."

I reluctantly set down the blanket I was folding and walk over to the shelf. It's mostly canned goods with some crackers and instant noodles. I consider grabbing a can of peaches, but then I catch sight of a box of granola bars. The oats will hold off my hunger longer than peaches, so I reach inside and take a few bars.

Bending down, Owen pulls out a small basket tucked under the shelf with several bottles of water. My hands are shaking when I reach for the bottle he holds out to me.

"Do you want to take the blanket too?" he asks. "It's still pretty chilly."

I give the thick wool blanket a long look but then slowly shake my head. "Thank you, but once I get moving, I'll be fine." I know once we get farther down the mountain I'll warm up, then I'll end up having to carry it the rest of the way to my camp.

He grunts his agreement and then leads me out of the cave and down a narrow trail that a mountain goat would look twice at, but this giant of a man walks down without a care in the world.

I don't remember it being this narrow and steep on the way up, so I carefully pick my way along behind him. Of course, last night, my mind was on the fact that I was draped over the shoulder of a mythical creature. A *very aroused* mythical creature.

"So, are you from around here?" Owen asks as he leads me down the side of the mountain.

"Um, no." I carefully place one foot in front of the other along the narrow path while keeping an eye on my surroundings, in case the bigfoot decides to come back. "I'm from Virginia."

"Virginia? That's about as far from here as you can get. What brought you this far?"

I know he's probably just making small talk, but part of me can't help but wonder if he's also fishing for information.

"I was born here. Well, actually in Vancouver, but we moved when I was a kid."

Owen looks back at me over his shoulder. "So, you're visiting family?"

Hmm, definitely fishing. "No. Just camping with friends."

When I don't elaborate, he turns back to watch where he's going, and we lapse into a surprisingly comfortable silence. That is, until I decide to do some fishing of my own.

"So how long have you been a park ranger?" I ask.

"Oh, ever since I graduated high school." He tosses me a smile over his shoulder.

"Did you always want to be a ranger? Or did you have other aspirations?"

We reach the end of the steepest part of the trail, and I'm thankful when it widens so I can walk beside him. "These mountains are in my blood." Owen lifts his dark eyes to roam across the sky and over the treetops before resting on me. "I've never wanted to do anything else."

A smile pulls at the corners of my lips. "I wish I felt that way about something."

"Oh? And what do you do?"

My nose wrinkles. "I'm a recruiter for a big insurance company."

"Oh."

"Yeah. *Oh* pretty much sums it up."

"If you hate it, why not find something else?"

"I don't *hate* it," I grumble. I don't love it either, but... "I'm good at it, and the pay and benefits are too good to turn down." I finish with a shrug.

I don't have much of a life outside work. Pretty much my only hobby is bigfoot. I don't have a lot of friends because I've never really felt like I fit in anywhere. Except, I feel like I could belong here. Even after being abducted by the very creature I was hoping to see. Something about the wide-open sky and crisp mountain air feels—

Don't say "like home."

As much as I love it here, when my time is up, I'll head back to Roanoke, and that will be it. I won't have any other excuse to come back again.

Owen nods like he understands, but I know he doesn't. How could he? He just said this is where he's always wanted to be.

"I think it's important to be happy, no matter where you're at or what you do," he glances at me and offers a small smile, "because when you're happy, everything else falls into place."

I think about that. Then I wonder—have I ever truly been happy? Like, the soul-deep content kind of happy? And suddenly I realize that's how I've felt ever since arriving here. Despite all the hiccups, like creepy Darren and being abducted by bigfoot, this place makes me truly happy. Which makes me kind of sad, since I can't stay. I quickly push that thought away to ponder another day, and not on the side of a mountain with a stranger.

"You should write self-help books," I say.

He chuckles. "I don't know about that. Most people don't care much for anything I have to say."

"Well, maybe they should."

"Maybe they should," he agrees.

CHAPTER EIGHT

J ust like last night, I was halfway back to my cabin before I was able to shift back.

Even though I make way better time as a squatch, with the daylight comes tourists who can pop up anywhere or at any time. Although awkward, at least now if someone catches me walking bare-ass naked, they'd likely avoid eye contact and move away. Giving them a story to share later, *'Y'all are not going to believe the walk of shame I saw on my hike today.'*

Turns out, I have bigger problems. Like the fact that the keys to my place were in my pocket when I squatched out in front of the campers, which means they are long-gone somewhere on the side of the mountain.

Climbing up onto my porch, my ears ring with Owen's nagging voice: *"Why don't you keep a spare key somewhere, like under the welcome mat?"*

Gritting my teeth, I silence his imagined voice with a well-aimed kick to the door, just under the knob. The second the wood splinters under my foot, I remember that I ran out so fast last night, I never locked the door behind me.

I want to bang my head against something as I carefully

close the ruined door behind me. Thanks to the broken lock, it doesn't want to latch anymore, so I brace it with the small table I keep my mail on. My dinner is still sitting beside my recliner, long gone cold, and the TV is on.

After the long night, and two shifts, I'm too tired to deal with clean-up, so I bypass it and walk straight to the back of the house and into my bedroom. Way beyond weary, I don't stop until the front of my thighs hit the edge of my bed, and then I just fall face first into the mattress. I'm out the moment my body stops moving and sleep like I'm dead until Owen comes pounding at my door sometime after noon.

It's not the pounding that wakes me so much as the crash of the busted door, followed by my brother's shouting. "What the fu—*Sean*, how many times do I have to tell you to get a spare key?"

Letting out a long, painful groan, I force myself out of my bed. I'm still naked, so I grab a pair of gray sweatpants lying beside my overflowing laundry basket. At the sound of my shuffled steps coming down the hallway, Owen gives me a brief glance, probably to make sure I'm dressed, as he tries to fix the broken door. Our houses were built around the same time and by the same builder, who built a dozen other homes for the park rangers to use. The only difference between mine and Owen's houses is that his has an extra guest room. Since he was the oldest, we just assumed he'd be the first of us to settle down and have a family, so he'd need more room.

How does that saying go? *The devil fools with the best-laid plans.*

Standing back, I watch my brother fuck with the broken latch until he finally gives up with a heavy sigh. He braces the small table against it, the way I had it, and heads for the kitchen.

"How did it go?" I follow after him, where he's already

head and shoulders deep in my fridge, reaching for a beer, only to find—

"What the fuck is this?" He holds up a colorful can pinched between his fingers like it might bite him.

"It's cider. So, what happened?"

"Nothing happened." Owen ducks back into the fridge. "Where's the fucking beer?"

"I ran out." Grabbing the can from him, I pop the top. "So nothing at all happened when you took Olivia back to her camp?"

"You think alcoholic apple juice is *better* than beer?"

I start to hand him the open can but then pull it away when he reaches out to take it. "First, tell me about Olivia."

Owen makes a face. "The girl was fine. Just a little shook up. She even went along with the bear story, which doesn't make sense if she's up there looking for squatch. I don't think we'll have any trouble from her."

I lower my arm, and he takes the can from me. Then, like a fucking kid trying something he's certain he won't like, he takes the tiniest, most tentative sip and makes a face.

"Fuck! This shit is awful." After slamming the fridge door shut, he storms back into the living room, where he falls into my recliner. Still gripping the can of cider, he wakes up my TV and starts scrolling until he finds the show I was trying to watch last night. Leaning back, he pops up the footrest and tilts the can back to take a long drink.

Without looking away from the TV, he says, "You should go check on those campers. Make sure they aren't making trouble."

This *motherfucker*. Coming into *my* home, stealing *my* cider, and then *my* chair and *my* TV—

"Why are you here?" I grit through clenched teeth. I've barely eaten. I haven't slept for more than a couple hours for the last two nights, and he thinks he can just order me around like a–

Owen turns and gives me a droll look. "You wanna stand there and tell me about why the campers saw your boner slapping between your thighs last night? Or maybe why her cave smelled like sex?"

My mouth snaps shut, and I drag my hand through my hair. Yeah, I definitely don't want to talk about *that*. He turns back to face the TV. "Then go see what they're up to."

And that's when I realize he's basically giving me an excuse to see Olivia again.

Well, I don't have to be told twice—or was it three times?

I hurry back to my bedroom to dress. Considering I squatched out the last two times I saw her, I don't bother picking anything nice. I simply throw on a t-shirt and shove my feet in a pair of slides I mostly wear around the house.

When I make my way back into the living room, my stomach lets out a mighty groan, so I make a quick lunch to eat on the way. Shifting usually makes me ravenous, and I've shifted twice now in the span of twelve hours.

Stomping past Owen, I pause long enough to shove my hand between the chair and into his pocket, grabbing his keys since mine were on the ring with my house key.

"Hey!" he shouts, but I just rattle them at him as I head out the door, not bothering to shut it behind me. I'll need to make a trip to town sooner rather than later to fix it.

"Call if you need anything," Owen shouts after me, and I flip him off before stepping down from my porch.

On my way up to the campsite, I decide to stop by the trailhead where I know Ben—the one who called Owen last night about the missing camper—is working.

Ben has been a park ranger since he got out of diapers, or at least that's how he likes to tell it. The old coot should have retired decades ago, but he just keeps showing up. Someday I'm sure I'll come check on him to find him finally taking the eternal nap, but that day is not today.

When I pull up, he pops his head out of the small ranger station—which is little more than a kiosk—with his signature smile and wave.

"Hey, Ben, how's it been today?" I lean into the window he keeps open so the tourists can ask him questions without him having to get up from his stool.

"Not bad, not bad," he says. "It's been kind of quiet." Reaching over me, he raps his knuckles against the wood sill. "Knock wood it stays that way."

I rest my chin on my folded hands. "Why wouldn't it stay that way?"

Ben's rheumy eyes shift to look behind me before he leans in to whisper—loudly, "Because there was another sighting."

I have to press my lips tightly closed to keep from smiling. "Oh? Another sighting of what?"

He looks around again, though there isn't anyone near us who might overhear, even if we're shouting. "You know, one of *those* sightings. A bigfoot sighting."

I lean back with a dry laugh. "Really, Ben? You don't believe that nonsense, do you?"

He gives me the most serious look I've ever seen from him, and my laugh quickly dies. "Look, son, I know you don't really believe these sightings are nonsense. In fact, I think you probably know more about the strange things that live in these mountains than any of us." He purses his dry, thin lips. "So don't go pissing on me and calling it rain."

This time, my laugh is genuine as I reach through the window and clap him on the shoulder. I should know better than to try to fool ol' Ben. Hell, he probably knows more about the native legends around here than I do—and I grew up with them.

He leans back on his stool. "Whatcha doing up here anyway? I heard you and Owen had a long night."

Yup. Good ol' Ben doesn't miss a thing. "I was just going to check on those campers. Is there anything I should know before I get there?"

Ben shakes his head. "They're mostly staying to themselves."

"Good." I rap my knuckles on the sill one more time and then step back with a wave. "See you around, Ben."

He waves after me, and I head back to Owen's truck. With my hand on the door, I pause and then change my mind, deciding the walk up to the campsite will be good for me.

By the time I make it up to Windy Ridge, my legs are burning, probably because I'm wearing a pair of slides and not sensible boots, and I'm covered in a light sheen of sweat. The sun is getting low on the horizon, but my attention is on the quiet campsite.

The campers are nowhere to be seen. Although their vehicle is still parked beside the line of tents curved around a central fire that is cold, so wherever they've gone, they'll be back. Likely they're just taking advantage of the view and some day hiking.

My steps are light as I make my way around the tents, peeking inside each one to make sure I'm not going to accidentally startle someone who might have stayed behind. But all the tents are empty. Including the last one. The one that makes me pause. Rocking back on my heels, I breathe in the sweet scent seeping through the nylon, savoring the way it makes my sinuses tingle and my head spin.

Against my will—or at least my better judgment—I unzip the door of the unassuming green tent. It's nothing fancy, just a basic dome tent. The kind you can buy just about anywhere.

Pulling back the mesh panel, I crouch down and stick my head inside. Everything is neat and tidy. Her sleeping bag is laid out on the left side, zipped up and resting on a blow-up sleeping pad. Her carry-on and a small electric lantern take up the other side, leaving a narrow space between the two.

Before I can stop myself, I crawl inside.

It's far too small to stand up in, so I'm forced to stay crouched as I snoop like a freaking creep. My nose twitches as I make my way over to her bed. When I run my hand over the silky sleeping bag material, a low rumble rolls through my chest. At the top of the bed is a small pillow that I pick up and bring to my nose.

It's saturated with her sweet scent. Peaches drizzled in honey and the flowery scent of her shampoo. My eyes slide closed, and I bury my face deeper into its softness as my pulse starts to pound in my dick.

I'm not sure how long I stay like this, but while I'm distracted, the sun sets, and darkness descends over the campground. But it's the sound of voices that jolts me from my—whatever the fuck I'm doing.

Shit! What the hell am I doing?

I toss the pillow away from me and turn to flee the tent, but it's too late. I can see the campers filing into their campsite through the mesh—which means there is no chance of sneaking out without being seen now.

Double shit!

Then I see *her*. Olivia is walking beside the bearded man. My eyes narrow. *Tony.*

A jealous snarl makes it way past my clenched teeth at the easy smile she gives him as they talk quietly. I can't look away as they come closer and closer. I can't stop analyzing the comfortable way she acts with him. She isn't trying to impress or flirt with him. Maybe they really are just friends.

When they reach the fire, they part ways. Tony heads toward his tent, and Olivia—my breath catches when she turns toward hers. *Toward me.*

I'm frozen. Completely taken by how beautiful she is. Her shoulder-length hair is tucked behind her ears, and she's wearing a lightweight jacket instead of the soft hoodie she had on last night. Her cheeks are rosy from her hike and —then I remember where I am.

How the fuck am I going to get out of this mess? She's almost to the tent, and I'm trapped with nowhere to hide.

Then my skin starts to itch, and the familiar tingle of my shift rolls over me—through me.

Oh no. No no no... this isn't happening!

The shift is seamless, shredding my clothes as I try to curl my hairy seven-foot frame into the small space. Ducking down so I'm roughly the same shape as the dome tent I'm taking up space in.

On the other side of the nylon, Olivia pauses when she reaches the doorway, and her long fingers fall through the mesh I left open. "Huh, I swear I closed this," she says quietly to herself before pushing through the opening and into the dark tent, where I blend well with the shadows.

She keeps her back to me and flips on the lantern. I blink against the sudden brightness, wondering how the hell she hasn't noticed me yet. Biting down on my bottom lip, I watch as she shrugs out of her jacket. Today she's wearing a pink t-shirt with a rhino that says, *Save the Chubby Unicorns.*

She turns around and freezes. Her brown eyes flare wide, and a soft gasp is the only sound that makes it past her lips before I lunge. Clamping my hand over her mouth, I swing her around so I can press her back against her soft bedding.

OLIVIA

CHAPTER NINE

Everything happens so fast.

One minute, I'm getting ready to have a little post-hike lie-down before dinner. The next, the tent is shaking as I'm swept off my feet and tossed onto my sleeping bag. Landing flat on my back, I blink up to find a monster hovering over my prone body. His shoulders are hunched so he doesn't bust out of the ceiling, and when I suck in a sharp breath to scream, his giant palm wraps around the bottom half of my face, leaving room under my nose so I can breathe.

I'm helpless as I stare up at him in shock.

Melted chocolate-brown eyes framed with thick, dark lashes stare down at me. His face is both animal and distinctly humanoid, with his wide brow, flat nose, and thick lips. My mind is spinning as I take in the long strands of reddish-brown fur, streaked through with strands of everything from blond to sable.

I recognize him immediately as the bigfoot that carried me up to the cave and...*left*.

A hot blush creeps into my cheeks, remembering exactly what else he left in the cave. And that the hand covering my mouth is the same one he used to stroke himself. Suddenly, my cheeks aren't the only part of me that's getting hot.

Bigfoot's nostrils flare.

Oh, God! He can't smell me, can he? I squeeze my eyes shut with embarrassment when another rush of heat coats my panties.

This can't be happening. And why am I not freaking out more? Am I being naive to think, because he hasn't hurt me so far, he won't? I drag a deep breath in through my nose, hoping that when I open my eyes I'll be alone in my sleeping bag, and all of this will have been an awful dream.

Counting slowly, I peek under one eyelid to find the bigfoot still hunched over me, staring down at me curiously.

Great.

I whimper when he shifts his weight and holds one finger up to his lips. Silently asking if I can be quiet.

Glancing over his shoulder to the doorway, I see Brian has the fire going. His back is to my tent, and I can't see anyone else around. What would happen if he suddenly turned around? With the lantern on and the door half open, there would be nothing blocking the sight of the bigfoot pinning me to my bed.

The prospect of being caught like this cools some of the unsettling arousal that burned moments ago. Remembering how he batted the guys away when they were trying to rescue me the last time, I worry he might actually hurt them if they catch him again.

Dragging my eyes from the tent's entrance, I nod.

His warm brown eyes flick back and forth across my face, like he's trying to decide if he can trust me. Then, slowly, he eases some of his weight off me. Tapping his finger to his lips again, reminding me to keep quiet, he pulls his hand away from my mouth.

My tongue darts out to lick away the salt that coats my lips from his palm, and his eyes drop to my mouth. His eyes darken and he makes a deep noise that sounds suspiciously like a moan, sending another wave of heat flaring between my legs.

What in the hell is wrong with me? This is not the time or place to get horny!

Carefully, trying not to make any sudden moves that might trigger any kind of instinct from him, I lift myself up on my elbows.

"You shouldn't be here," I whisper, darting another nervous glance at the doorway. I need to figure out how to get him out of here before anyone notices.

Outside the tent, Tony has joined Brian at the campfire. They both have their backs to me, and neither has noticed what's going on in my tent.

Bigfoot's lips quirk up at the corners in a smirk when this is *not* a smirk-worthy situation!

"This isn't funny!" I hiss.

He starts to lean over me again, and this time, I have the presence of mind to scoot out from under him, which earns me a deep frown.

"How am I going to get you out of here without the guys seeing you?" I ask, glancing around for something that might hide him. Which is laughable since he barely fits in my tent as it is. I look back at him again. "What are you doing here, anyway?"

Of course he doesn't answer. Seems that for all the intelligence I see in his warm brown eyes, he lacks the ability to do more than grunt.

This is a disaster.

I rub at the tension headache that has sprung up behind my eyes.

"Hey, Liv. Did we eat all the hotdogs last night?" Tony

shouts from outside, making me jump and clamp my hands over my mouth to hold back a startled scream.

Bigfoot's smirk falls away, and every inch of his muscular body tenses.

"Liv?" Tony calls out again.

It takes me a minute to realize Tony has moved over by the SUV, where he's digging through the cooler we keep in the back. He hasn't noticed what's going on in my tent yet.

I glance up at Bigfoot. Right now would be the perfect time to call for help. When I open my mouth, his eyes narrow and his body tenses.

"Um, no," I shout back, trying to keep my voice as neutral as possible, "I think I saw Darren snag them for lunch, though."

Tony's shoulders sag with his disappointment.

Bigfoot also slumps, but with relief.

Tony pushes himself back from the cooler and my heart speeds up when I think that he might come back to the fire.

Don't turn around. Don't turn around. Don't turn—

He goes back to digging through the cooler as he mutters, "Kabobs it is, then."

I shift my attention back to Bigfoot. "Okay, we need to get you out of—"

Before I have a chance to say more, he reaches for me.

"Oh, no—"

Huge, strong hands circle my waist, and I bite back a scream when he lifts me off my sleeping bag and clutches me to his chest. I open my mouth to... to what? To argue with him? To scream? Fighting him is useless, and I'm having trouble remembering why I even want to.

I feel safe with him, even though I probably shouldn't. I keep coming back to the fact that he hasn't hurt me. Or given me any indication that he wants to hurt me.

He forced you to watch him jack off after kidnapping you

and taking you to a cave! A tiny voice reminds me. *If that's not a red flag...*

Except I was hardly *forced*. I could have closed my eyes or looked away anytime. If he's as intelligent as I think he is, I could have asked him to stop. But I didn't. No, I watched every stroke, and I got wet from it. So, who is the real creeper?

"Why do you keep doing this?" I ask him quietly.

Bigfoot goes still. His eyes fill with *uncertainty*, and slowly, he shakes his head.

"You don't know? But...you're not going to hurt me, are you?"

His eyes blaze, and he shakes his head harder.

Relief washes over me. "And you won't hurt the guys?"

His lip curls up into a sneer as he glances over his shoulder before turning back to me to shake his head a third time.

"Okay." I'm not sure what I'm agreeing to exactly, but I don't fight him when he ducks out of my tent and steps directly into the middle of our camp. I know it's probably too much to ask, but I can't help hoping that maybe no one will notice us.

"What the fuck?"

I don't look to see who says it, and it doesn't matter. We've been seen.

I should be pleading with him to put me down. To let me go. But I know it's useless—*and* I don't really want him to. So instead, I press my palm against his chest, look up at him and say, *"*You'd better run.*"*

He sweeps my legs up, so he's carrying me bridal style, and lopes away from the campsite and into the trees. Just like he did the night before.

SEAN

CHAPTER TEN

My chest is tight, and I'm struggling through a case of déjà vu as I hike up the ridge with Olivia cradled in my arms. At least this time, she isn't wriggling and screaming. And my cock isn't hanging out, although it is throbbing like it's got its own heartbeat inside my sheath.

Owen is going to kill me when he finds out that I've kidnapped her again.

Can it be called kidnapping when she went willingly?

Why can't I seem to leave this woman alone? What is it about her that has me so captivated? I press my nose to her hair and take a deep breath, letting her wildflowers and honey scent coat the inside of my nose. *There has to be something else going on that I don't understand.*

I was sixteen when I lost my parents in a car accident, so I never really got the birds and bees and squatch talk from my pop. Owen tried to fill in for our parents, but he was busy building a life for us, doing his best to keep me out of trouble and on the right path.

With no close family around, it's not like I could ask anyone else. Owen gave me the basic *no glove, no love* talk, and we were both happy to leave it at that. Until now. I wonder if Owen even knows. It's not like he's dated much. The poor guy is a workaholic.

Olivia weighs next to nothing in my arms as I make my way up the steep incline. She's taking this far better than she should be and staying incredibly calm. Not just calm, but relaxed. Her head is resting against my chest as she gently twirls my long hair around her fingers. She surprises me even more when she leans in and *sniffs me*.

My steps slow, and she seems embarrassed when she looks up at me. "Sorry," she says quietly. "Was that weird?"

I can only grunt softly. Yeah, it's a little weird, but I don't mind. I like the idea of her scenting me.

She goes back to twirling my fur around her finger. "I've always heard stories that bigfoot sightings are preceded by a rank smell. Suggesting they have a potent aroma. But you..." she leans in and presses her nose to my chest again, breathing deeply, "you smell really nice. Like the outdoors after a hard rain, earthy and fresh."

My cock jumps, and I can't hold back my low groan as it springs from my sheath, bobbing from side to side in time with my strides.

Just great. At least Olivia can't see what's happened below her. I've never been unable to control myself around a woman before.

Taking a deep breath, I try to think of gutting fish and long days working in the torrential downpours that frequent the mountains in winter. I grit my teeth and imagine how pissed Owen is going to be with me. Anything to keep my mind off how good Olivia feels pressed against me. Or how her sweet scent goes straight to my head with each breath I take. I certainly don't need to be thinking of how soft her breasts feel pressed against my chest. Or how much I like that she keeps touching my fur and sniffing me.

I'm so focused on the woman in my arms that I'm not paying any attention to where I'm going. It's not until I find myself climbing the steps to my house that realize I've taken myself home.

"Oh." She turns away from my chest to take in the old rambler. The porch light illuminates the peeling paint and cobwebs, giving the house an abandoned look, and I want to defend it. It's due for a fresh coat of paint and could use some remodeling for sure, but it's solidly built.

When she doesn't start squirming or trying to escape my arms, I step up onto the creaky porch. Owen must have rigged the door to stay shut when he left, but a nudge from my toe is enough for it to fall open. Trying not to think of the symbolism of carrying her over the threshold in my arms, I set Olivia on her feet just inside the door.

Her head swivels as she takes in my plain living room. "Whose place is this? Will they be back soon?"

There's no way to know when Owen left, but I notice my OCD brother cleaned up after himself. And me. The place is far tidier than I left it.

Olivia stares up at me with curiosity and confusion as I take her hand and lead her over to my recliner. Reaching around her, I hand her the remote and then gently push her down so she's sitting.

"Well, this is an improvement from the cave," she says with a smirk. "I'd say you're getting better at this kidnapping thing."

With my hands in front of my hips, where my cock hasn't quite slipped back inside its sheath, I slowly back away.

Her smile falls. "Wait. You're leaving me here?"

I shouldn't have taken her from the camp in the first place. *But I don't like her being alone with all those other men*. By bringing her here, I know she's safe and surrounded by my scents.

When I step through the open door, Olivia jumps up from my chair. "Wait! Don't go. I need to get back to my camp—" But I'm already pulling the door closed between us.

Before I can talk myself into staying, I hurdle the railing that wraps around the porch and lope into the forest. I don't stop running until I've worked myself right up to the point of exhaustion. Only then does my squatch finally let go of his grip on me, letting me slide back into my human form. By then it's been hours, and I'm miles from anything.

It's a long walk back down the mountain. By the time I find myself climbing the steps to Owen's cabin, it's getting close to dawn. I'm naked *again* and shivering from the cold when I lift my hand to pound my fist on his door, but it opens before I have a chance.

"There you are," Owen sighs. Is that relief I hear in his voice? He's rocking bedhead, but he's still wearing his clothes from earlier, which means he must have been waiting for me. I'm too tired to fight with him about staying up for me like I'm a fucking teenager. The only thing I want right now is a hot shower and a place to crash since I left Olivia in my house.

I start to push past him, but he stops me with a warm hand on my shoulder. "Wait, I need to warn you—"

My nostrils twitch when a familiar sweetness drifts through his door. My hand moves before my brain gives the signal, and I wrap my fingers around my brother's throat, pushing him backward so he's pressed to the doorjamb. I search the space for the woman responsible for the scent.

A snarl rumbles from between my teeth as I dig my nails into the sides of his neck. "*She's mine!*"

"Calm the fuck down, Sean," Owen chokes around my grip. "You'll wake her, and she *just* fell asleep."

That's when I see Olivia curled up into a tight little ball on Owen's couch, with a plush blanket covering her.

"What is she doing here?" Seeing her in my brother's house instead of *mine* has my skin crawling again. But for once, I don't shift. I'm too worn out, I think. Owen pries my fingers from around his throat.

"When I didn't hear from you after sending you to check on the campers, I called your sat phone, and *she* answered." He points to Olivia. "Why the fuck was she in your house? And where the fuck were you?"

I really don't want to do this right now. Mostly because I know everything I've done regarding this woman has been wrong. And also because I'm naked and freezing. And exhausted.

When I don't answer, Owen keeps going. "I went and got her with the quad–since you had my truck. I brought her back here, fed her, and then made her a spot on the couch while we waited for you to turn up so you could take her back to her campsite."

Owen shakes his head. "I should have known you squatched out again. And where is my truck now? Back at the trailhead? Or ditched in the forest?"

Not wanting to admit I left it back at the trailhead, I grit my teeth, but that doesn't stop them from chattering.

Suddenly, Owen's pissed-off expression turns to worry. "Fuck, how long have you been naked?" He drags me inside and closes the door behind me. The way I'm shivering, I think I might be on the verge of being hypothermic. Our squatch is impervious to cold, but our human bodies are not.

"D-d-d-don't-t-t kn-n-n-n-n—"

Owen pushes me toward the bathroom, grabbing a towel out of the linen closet on the way. "Take a shower and get warm. I'll get the guest room ready for you when you're done. Then you're going to sleep, and we'll talk about this tomorrow."

Before I can argue with him, he pushes me through the doorway and shuts me inside.

I stand under the hot spray until my body temperature rises to an acceptable level, and then until the hot water runs cold. Only then do I dry myself and dress in the sweats Owen left me to sleep in.

The house is dark when I let myself out of the bathroom, and I start to cross the hallway to the guest room, only my feet take me to the left. Back into the living room, past the couch where Olivia is sleeping soundly, to the loveseat across from her.

I'm twice as long as it, but I curl my frame into it anyway, pulling a quilt draped across the back to cover myself. With my head resting on a too-firm decorative pillow, I watch my woman sleep.

She's not mine.

Yes. She is.

My head throbs as my splintered mind argues with itself over the woman across from me. I'm not sure how long I watch her, but the eastern sky is starting to lighten when my eyes finally drift shut, and they don't open again.

OLIVIA

CHAPTER ELEVEN

A dull ache in my lower back drags me from the deep sleep I was enjoying. Rolling onto my back, I stretch it out so I can go back to sleep, but the moment my eyes flutter open, I realize I'm not in my tent. All hope of going back to sleep disappears.

I really need to stop waking up in strange places.

The same park ranger who brought me down from the cave came to my rescue again last night. But instead of taking me back to the campsite, he brought me to his house. We were waiting for Owen's brother to return with his truck, then he was supposed to take me back, but obviously that didn't happen. Tony and Brian are probably freaking out.

I take in the rustic room and note the differences between Owen's house compared to the house Bigfoot brought me to. The thick stained beams that stretch across the ceiling and the clean white walls are nearly identical. So is the fact that there isn't much for wall hangings. But Owen's furniture all matches, and his front door isn't hanging off its hinges. The other house was definitely someone's bachelor pad.

The leather couch creaks under me, and the bare skin on my arm sticks, making a *flllppp* sound when I roll to my side. I start to push myself up to sit when I notice the smaller couch across from me is occupied. At first, I think it's Owen who's barely contained within the much-too-small loveseat. But I quickly realize that, unless Owen suddenly aged backward and lightened his hair, it can't be him.

The man is stretched out on his stomach, with one leg hanging over the side and the other stretched over the armrest. His face is turned toward me, with one arm curled tightly against his chest and the other stretched out so it's hanging over the opposite armrest like his leg. A quilt is bunched around his waist. I lick my lips as I take in all the tanned skin covering his strong muscles, then scold myself for staring at him like that.

Even deeply asleep, this man looks exhausted. Bruised circles shadow where thick dark lashes fan across his cheeks. The way his neck is cranked up at an angle makes me wince—he's going to be sore when he wakes.

His breaths are deep and even as I watch him from across the room. His nose hooks slightly at the end and his brows are thicker in the center before tapering at both ends, both identical to Owen's features.

This must be the brother he told me about. And also, *damn...* Owen is a good-looking guy, but his brother might be the most beautiful man I've ever set eyes on.

They share similar angular faces with high cheekbones and a chiseled jaw, but this man's tousled hair is a longer, lighter brown with streaks of blond and red instead of silver. My fingers itch to brush away the strands that have fallen across his closed eyes. To lightly stroke along his jaw that is shadowed by a few days' growth of beard. Would his skin feel soft or bristled?

"Good morning," Owen says as he passes in front of the couch on his way to the kitchen.

I jump, clutching at my chest as heat rushes into my face at being caught staring at his sleeping brother.

"Do you want some coffee?" he asks, not realizing the mini-heart attack he just gave me. "I have some milk and sugar, but none of that fancy stuff."

I glance back at the sleeping man and let out a relieved sigh. If Owen caught me ogling his brother, at least he's being polite enough not to mention it.

I push myself up so I'm sitting with both feet on the floor. "Um, coffee and milk would be great. Thank you."

I'm still in my clothes from yesterday, and I nervously run my fingers through my messy hair. I've never been good around strangers and strange places. Even when I was a kid, I was usually the one begging to be picked up early from a slumber party. The awkwardness of waking up in Owen's home, where I'm at the whim of his unfamiliar routine has my heart fluttering.

A few minutes later, Owen returns to the living room and hands me a steaming mug with a USFS emblem on the side. He's carrying a matching mug.

"Did you sleep alright?" He falls back into his leather recliner.

"Yes. Thank you." I blow across the top of the milky coffee before taking a sip. I can't help my satisfied hum when the warm bitterness hits my tongue. "Thank you for letting me crash here, but I should probably get back to camp. My friends are going to be worried."

"Uh... about that." Owen's face scrunches up. "When Sean finally showed up, he didn't have my truck with him."

I glance at the man still fast asleep across from me. "Is that's your brother?"

Owen nods.

"And... how did he get here if he didn't have your truck?" My heart starts beating faster at the prospect of being stuck here even longer.

There is no missing the irritated look Owen shoots the sleeping man. "I have a feeling he left it at the trailhead. As for how he got here, he walked."

My forehead scrunches up as I try to figure out how... and why...

"Was he... drunk?" I ask, eyeing the sleeping man again. He looks like he could be sleeping off a bender, but there are no alcoholic fumes coming off him.

"No, no. Sean hardly drinks at all. He just hasn't slept in a couple days," Owen explains. Only, it explains nothing.

A feeling of relief flows out of me that this gorgeous man isn't a drunk. Holding the mug up to my face, I let my eyes flick back to Sean. *Why can't I quit looking at him?*

Owen offers an apologetic smile. "Nothing short of a bomb is going to wake him anytime soon. But once he's up, I'll have him take you back."

I lean back into the couch with a frustrated sigh. "I appreciate everything, but... I really need to get back soon."

Owen's eyes flick back and forth between me and his brother, and his expression turns... *thoughtful*. "You've met him before, you know."

I snort. "I think I'd remember meeting him." *Oh god, did that sound as pervy as I think it did?*

Owen smirks at me across his mug. "Don't be so sure about that."

I'm getting the strangest feeling that he's trying to tell me something without actually telling me, like he's hinting at an inside joke that I don't get and it's frustrating as hell.

Just then, the man in question shifts with a low groan. The last of the quilt slides off him to pool on the floor as he rolls to his back. I bite down on my bottom lip as I take in the way a pair of worn sweats ride low on his narrow hips. With a deep groan, he stretches out his long frame at the same time he reaches down to scratch at his balls.

My mouth goes dry and my eyes are locked on the sight of those sweatpants being pulled even lower. Enough to give me a brief glimpse of dark hair and the hint of a thick shaft that's growing thicker as it rises to attention before my eyes.

He lets out a soft moan and guides his hand from his balls to grip himself through the gray material. My stomach flip-flops, and I squeeze my thighs together, biting down harder on my lip to keep from moaning with him.

His hips hitch, and he starts a slow stroke—

"Sean! We've got company!" Owen barks suddenly.

I'm sure my whole face is tomato red when Sean freezes and his eyes snap open. They are a rich chocolate brown and *familiar,* though I can't place why. His Adam's apple bobs with a swallow, and he slowly turns his head toward me.

Our eyes meet and it's like being in the center of a tornado. All I feel is calm, while everything around me is swirling chaos. All my embarrassment and nervousness slips away like sand in the wind.

The calm doesn't last, though, because suddenly he begins to tremble. Those melty chocolate eyes turn frightened and then frantic, as the trembling turns to shaking.

"Sean, don't—" I hear Owen warn him. But it's too late.

One second, Sean is draped across the loveseat. The next there is a seven-foot bigfoot in his place.

CHAPTER TWELVE

Except for the sound of wood splintering and the rushing blood in my ears, the room is quiet. Then I notice Olivia's soft breathing followed by Owen swearing.

Jesus fucking Christ.

Slowly, I swing my legs around so I'm sitting upright. My weight crushed the springs, so my knees are now at the same level as my armpits, and my hands are awkwardly resting on my thighs. I keep my gaze on the floor so I can't see the fear I'm certain is burned into Olivia's face.

Why does this keep happening? I've never had trouble controlling my shift before. What is it about Olivia that makes me squatch out every time I get close to her?

My nose twitches, and I expect to be hit with the bitter tang of her fear... but there is none. My brows knit, and when I look up, I'm not sure what surprises me more, the curious and unafraid expression on her face, or the fact that she's smiling.

"This definitely explains some things," she says with a breathy laugh before she glances over at Owen. "Um, so, if you're brothers, can you do this too?"

There is a long pause. "Yeah," Owen admits. "It's sort of a family thing."

She turns her wide eyes back at me. "Are there a lot of you in your family?"

"Just the two of us around here," Owen answers for us. "The gene is passed down through our father's line, so we have some cousins up and down the coast who have also inherited it."

"But," her shapely brows drop low over her eyes, "but there are so many sightings. Not just here, but all around the world."

"Ours isn't the only family who carries the gene," Owen says into his mug as he takes a sip.

Olivia leans back into the couch, her coffee forgotten in her lap, as she considers this. I can practically see her mind working on questions, debating what to ask first.

"So, is this," she waves between Owen and me, "an '*if I tell you, I'll have to kill you*' situation?"

Owen laughs. Probably harder than I've seen him laugh in a long time. Watching this woman break my overly serious brother out of his shell... I get the strangest sense that she belongs here, in our world.

But with me, because she's mine.

"No, it's not that kind of situation," Owen assures her. "But we do have to ask for secrecy. You can imagine what might happen if any of this got out."

The color in her cheeks fades, and her expression turns serious.

"Yeah. I understand." She looks back at me and stays quiet for a long time before she nods, like she's come to a decision. "I promise not to ever tell anyone about any of this." Then the corner of her lips turns down. "But what am I going to tell the guys? They might buy my story once, but they saw you twice... I'm not sure I'll be able to lie my way out of that."

Pinned under her concerned gaze, I'm captivated. Not just by her beauty, although I can't ignore the way my body reacts to hers. It's more than just attraction. The way she's accepting this...she's like a puzzle piece I didn't realize was missing, and I want to find out where her piece fits with mine.

Except, I remind myself, she's just another tourist with no plans to stick around. For my own wellbeing, I need to slam the door shut on whatever this longing is, because it's only going to hurt more when she leaves.

"I'm mostly worried about your friend Darren," Owen says with a sigh.

Olivia scrunches her nose up. "He's not really a friend," she admits. "I just met him two days ago, and he's mostly kept to himself." She scrunches up her nose as she looks from Owen to me. "To be honest, there's something he said the first night I met him that I haven't been able to forget. He told us that a bigfoot killed his brother."

A tremble runs through my body when her eyes flick to mine.

"That–that doesn't really happen, right?" she asks, her tone turning hopeful. "I mean, you'd never..."

She trails off when Owen and I share a knowing glance.

"Uh. Well..." Owen sets his mug aside and leans forward. "Despite our abilities, we *are* human, and humans can be provoked to make bad decisions. Humans can also do bad things without being provoked. We do our best to police our kind, to keep things like that from happening, but I would be lying if I said it didn't. But it's very rare."

The way she deflates at his answer sends a rush of irritation through me. I don't want her to think Owen and I could ever hurt her, or her friends. Suddenly, the itching is back, and it intensifies until my skin is quivering under my fur.

The change is so fast, I almost don't notice at first. The look on Olivia's face and the way her soft brown eyes suddenly spring wide is what makes me look down to see that I'm me again.

At least my shift didn't shred the sweats I'm wearing this time. Although, it stretched the already too big material, so it fits even looser around my hips and legs. I let out a low grumble when I think about how my next paycheck is going to go toward replacing clothes, doors, and keys.

"What's it like when that happens?" Olivia's eyes are bright with curiosity as she leans forward with her knuckles tucked under her chin.

"It doesn't feel like anything," I say honestly. I'm not sure how else to explain it. "One minute, I'm a squatch; the next I'm not."

"But how?"

I open my mouth, but then turn to Owen for help. He's much better at these types of things than I am.

"The way our dad explained it to us when we were kids was that it's similar to metamorphosis. Kind of like how a caterpillar changes into a butterfly. Only much faster, and we can go back and forth."

Olivia nods, but her brows stay tightly knit.

"That's the closest scientific explanation," I add, "but the easiest way to understand is to believe there is real magic in this world, and this is an example of it."

Understanding lights up her face.

Owen pushes himself up in his chair. "Sean, before you woke up, Olivia was telling me that she needs to get back to camp." He takes her empty mug and turns a hard look at me. "And when you get my truck, I have a list of things we need from town."

I'm surprised he's offering to let me make the weekly trip into town since that's usually his thing, so he can go stare at his girl or whatever he does. Owen has been panting after Jenny ever since she moved here and took over the general store. I've long suspected there is something going on between them, but I have no idea what's keeping them from sealing whatever the deal is.

"Right," I grit out. "I gotta steal more of your clothes though."

"Just try not to shred them this time. And fill the tank before you head back! If you're going to keep stealing my truck, at least put gas in it when you're done."

BY THE TIME I finish getting dressed, Owen has two travel mugs filled with steaming coffee waiting for me, and Olivia is nibbling on a bagel slathered in thick cream cheese. I do a double take when I see she's wrapped in one of his thick flannel shirts, and my skin prickles at seeing her in my brother's clothing.

She should be wrapped in my *clothes, not my brother's.*

A low growl slips past my throat before I can swallow it down. When Olivia gives me a wary look, I remind myself that she was only in a t-shirt and jeans when I took her from her tent. It shouldn't matter whose flannel she's wearing, as long as she's warm. Our eyes meet for a moment, and she quickly looks down at the bagel she's holding.

Damnit! I open my mouth to explain to her that I'm not angry, least of all at her, just as Owen strides into the room with a handwritten list for me. "If you can't find everything, just give the list to Jenny, and she can—"

I snatch the folded piece of paper. "I know how to fucking shop."

With a long sigh, I reach around Olivia and open the door. "Ready to go?" I try to lighten my tone, but she keeps her head down when she nods and strides past me and down the steps.

As the house falls away behind us, she hands me one of the travel mugs and then produces a second bagel.

"Thank you." I try to catch her eye, but she won't look at me.

Fuck! I really screwed up.

A thick, tense silence envelops us while we walk, and I scramble to think of what to say to her. It will take about an hour to reach the trailhead, and the last thing I want is to spend the whole thing in silence. I'd give anything to know what she's thinking, so I can better tailor what I want to say to her. But things like this are never that easy.

"Olivia, I'm sor–" I begin to apologize at the same time she asks, "Can you tell me about your kind? About bigfoots?"

The thought of telling her even more about my kind, and then watching her walk away twists my guts. But she already knows most of it anyway, so she might as well know it all. Besides, I'd rather she have the correct information, rather than making up her own assumptions.

"Well, for one thing, we don't call ourselves bigfoots. Or bigfeet or any other kind of big..." I try to keep my words lighthearted, but she ducks her head again.

"Sorry, is it sasquatch, then?"

"That's closer." I can't stop staring at her while we walk. I wish she would look up at me. My fingers twitch, wanting to curl my much larger hand around hers. "We're known as *sasqu'ets* throughout most of North America. It's a Salish word that means *hairy man*. Of course, different tribes and cultures have their own names and variations. Mostly we just call ourselves squatch."

"And where do they—do you—come from?" Her voice is soft, and when she finally looks up at me, her expression is filled with curiosity.

"We didn't come from anywhere," I say softly. "We've been here from the beginning. In the early times, it was more accepted that some of us were *different*. Now," I let out a sigh," it's much harder. There are more people. The stories aren't passed down like they used to be. Science tries to explain everything and disregards what it can't as fiction."

Silence falls over us again as she considers this. This time, the quiet that descends around us is filled with the sounds of birds and wildlife and the wind rustling through the trees. It's no longer heavy with the worry that I felt a few minutes ago, although I still find myself wondering if she can be trusted. So far, she hasn't given me a reason to distrust her, but...what if she tells someone else, and they go public?

Then there will be a bit of press, and it will eventually go away. Just like it always does.

I *want* to trust her, but I don't *know* her.

A voice in the back of my mind scoffs. *Then get to know her!*

No doubt Olivia would think I'm crazy if she could hear the way I'm arguing with myself. I start to laugh, and then try to stifle it, which turns into a snort, and she looks at me curiously.

"So, ah, what about you?" I clear my throat, like I meant to make the awkward noise.

"What about me?" She looks completely perplexed. Like she can't imagine that I would want to get to know her. Fuck, she's adorable.

"What brings you here, besides bigfoot?"

"Oh, um..." She tucks a strand of her straw-colored hair behind her ear and shrugs. "That's the reason, mostly."

I have my doubts, but if she doesn't want to talk about it, I'm not going to push her. So instead, I ask her about what she wants to talk about. "Then why did bigfoot bring you here?"

She keeps her eyes fixed on the trail we're following as her cheeks turn pink. "Well, I had a sighting, you know? I'm sure you don't want to hear about it. It seems kind of silly now, knowing what I know."

"Actually, I'd like to hear about it," I admit it honestly. "Tell me about your sighting, Olivia."

Her name on my tongue feels good, and when she looks up at me, her smile is back, along with the sparkle in her eyes. Sharing this is important to her, and if talking about bigfoot keeps that look on her face, then I'll listen all day long.

"I was seven when my family visited St. Helens," she begins.

I watch her intently as she tells me about getting lost in the dense forest. My heart pangs as the memory of her fear flickers across her face. I'm mesmerized by her excitement when she tells me how the squatch led her back to her family, and my stomach flutters along with her embarrassed flush when she admits that her sighting sparked her obsession and how long she's been planning to come back here.

"My parents were older when I was born, and I was their only child. I was in college when I lost them, one right after the other." She lets out a shaky breath and drops her gaze to the path again. "That was a rough time. They were the only family I had. I know they didn't mean for it to be like that for me, but taking care of them and school was pretty much my whole life for a really long time. So, my only friends were the ones I made online. Like Tony."

Hearing that, I decide that maybe Tony might not be so bad after all.

"Anyway, I was born here. In Washington, I mean, and I've always felt like something has been trying to pull me back. I used to think it was bigfoot, but..." She looks up at me and then around the lush forest we're walking through. "But I think it's just this place. Being here feels like home."

Olivia grows quiet again, and this time I let it stretch for a bit while enjoying the comfort of walking beside her, wondering which of my cousins she ran into that fateful day when she was seven.

"You know," I begin slowly. "Squatch don't show themselves to just anyone. They have to have a really good reason, so the fact that one helped you means..." I look over at her, and my heart kicks in my chest at the way the dappled sunlight is shining across her face. Our eyes meet, and warmth floods my body at the way the sun turns her eyes from warm brown to blazing amber.

She smiles up at me and—*my God, she's beautiful.* For a minute, I worry I'm about to squatch out again, but when nothing happens, I continue.

"It means he saw something special in you. That he could trust you."

I let what I just said sink into my own thick head, then I add, "I'm sorry about your parents." Shoving my hands into my pockets, I let out a long breath. Losing our parents when we were young is a hell of a thing to have in common. "I lost mine in an accident. They were driving in bad weather and..." I shrug.

Her fingers squeeze around my arm, and when I look over at her, her eyes have turned shiny with unshed tears. Her sadness for me and for my loss is unexpected. My heart swells in my chest, and I realize that if I ever look back on this moment, no matter what happens after today, *this* is the moment I'll remember as the first time I started to fall in love.

Our steps slow, and my eyes drop to her lips. I want to kiss her. To find out if she tastes as sweet as she smells.

My feet shuffle to a stop.

My heart jumps as her plush lips part with her next breath and her head tilts back so she's looking up at me. Taking another step, I close the distance between us. Electricity snaps down my spine when our hands brush. We're so close that our chests are nearly touching. I'm looking down at her, while she looks up. The tip of her small, pink tongue darts out to wet her lips and I swallow down a groan as I lean in to press my lips to hers. It's tentative, a feather-soft brush, like a question.

Is this okay?

Fuck yes, she answers when she leans in, pressing her lips firmly to mine.

Her hands glide up my arms to my shoulders, and I curl mine around her back, pulling her against me. She opens for me with a sigh and I sink inside the warmth of her mouth. Moaning at how she's just as sweet as I imagined. She tastes like coffee with a hint of honey and a flavor that is all her.

I groan, savoring the feel of her soft curves pressed against my hardness. My tongue dips and slides with hers. Her hands roam higher, up to the back of my neck, where she presses, asking for more. And I oblige, pulling her closer, wanting to feel every inch of her against every inch of me.

Our kiss turns hungry. Olivia meets my tongue with brazen flicks, and her blunt nails dig into the back of my neck. Holding her tightly, I grind my aching cock against her soft stomach.

Until the sudden sound of voices breaks me out of my reverie. Olivia tenses against me and *reluctantly* I pull back. Her eyes are glazed, and her lips are plump from my kisses.

Fuck, I want to kiss her again. Actually, I want to do far more than that.

I push aside thoughts of how she'll look spread out across my bed as I taste every inch of her bare skin. Gathering what's left of my willpower, I take her hand and twine our fingers together. We walk the rest of the way in silence.

Just ahead is the trailhead where Owen's old forestry truck is waiting in the parking lot, right where I left it. It's about two decades past its prime, but the thing runs like a dream thanks to my brother's handiwork. Owen is a genius around a motor. I always told him that he should have gone into some kind of engineering field, but he would just rattle off some bullshit about how his heart is here in the mountains.

After running my hand under the wheel well where he hides the spare key—I know because he's told me that's where he hides it a million times—I unlock the passenger side and help Olivia up into the cab. Then I take my time circling to the other side. Giving myself a pep-talk about how I am *not* going to squatch out the moment I'm closed up inside the cab with her. It's unneeded though; I seem to have my control back.

I make a mental note to ask Owen about it later. Maybe he can help me figure out what caused me to lose control in the first place.

As I pull out of the lot and onto the narrow trail that will take us up to Windy Ridge, Olivia shrugs out of Owen's flannel. When it starts to slide off the seat and onto the floor, we both reach for it, but I'm faster. With a growl, I snatch it from her and toss it behind the seat.

"Next time when you're cold, you can have my shirt."

She looks at me strangely and then points at the t-shirt I'm wearing. Her lips quirk up at the corners. "Isn't that Owen's shirt too?"

Shit. She has a point. "Yeah, but at least it's covered in my scent."

"Um, that's alright." She presses her lips tightly together, probably to keep from laughing at how ridiculous I'm acting. "Thank you, though." Then she does something I'm not expecting at all. She reaches over and twines her fingers with mine.

The drive up to the campsite flies by, even though I'm purposely driving slowly. I tell myself it's so I don't jostle her too much over the rough trail, but really I'm just dragging out the time until I have to let her go. My hand tightens around hers when I roll up next to the SUV. Before I've even come to a full stop, Tony and Brian are rushing at the truck.

My hand tightens around the steering wheel, and I'm seconds away from slamming the truck into gear and driving back down the mountain. But before I can make good on that, the door opens, and Tony pulls Olivia away from me. Her fingers slip from my grip, and then he's helping her down from the cab.

Her brows are puckered when she pulls away from Tony and turns back to look up into the cab. She smiles at me, "Thanks for the ride."

Before I can reply, Tony narrows his eyes and slams the door shut. Cutting off my view of her.

It's probably a good thing the windows are the old-fashioned crank kind, or who knows what stupid shit I would have shouted after him. Instead, I grind my teeth as I watch Brian and him walk Olivia back to the fire.

Slamming the truck into reverse, I try not to spray dirt and gravel as I turn around and head back down the mountain. At least until I'm out of view, then I open up the throttle and use speed to burn off the aggression I'm feeling at leaving her behind.

CHAPTER THIRTEEN

Slouched down into a camp chair in front of the smoldering fire, I can't stop thinking about Sean. My fingertips absently brush across my still tingling lips. The kiss we shared has been running through my mind on a loop that alternates with a flare of anger and then embarrassment.

I wasn't ready for our time together to be up, but then Tony and Brian were dragging me out of the truck, and Sean was driving away without so much as a wave.

"That was rude!" I'd snarled, spinning around and then shoving Tony away from me.

I've been sitting here ever since, rethinking the conversation Sean and I had while we walked. He was so attentive, looking at me like he actually cared about what I was saying, even the crazy bigfoot stuff. And then... when he kissed me...

Tony and Brian had to ruin all of it.

"Hey, Liv?!" Tony says loudly, like it wasn't the first time he tried to get my attention.

"What?" I snap at him. Then I close my eyes and take a deep breath. "Sorry, my mind is just miles away today."

"It's okay." Tony gives me a crestfallen look as he scoots his camp chair closer to mine, so he can lean in and talk to me without anyone overhearing. "Do you want to talk about it?"

He's already apologized a hundred times for pulling me out of Sean's truck the way he did, but I don't think he really is. Just like I don't think he's here to talk about Sean. At least the human version of him.

"There's not much to talk about," I say, just as Brian appears from behind me and sits on my other side with Darren appearing a moment later.

"Girl, you were carried off by a bigfoot—*twice, in as many days*. We've been dying to find out what happened to you." Brian says.

I knew the guys wouldn't leave me alone unless I told them *something* about last night. I can't tell them the truth, obviously. My mind races to come up with something believable enough so they won't question it. Because when I promised not to expose Sean and Owen for what they really are, I meant it.

"I have some terrible news for you," I begin. "There really is no such thing as bigfoot."

"How can you say that?" Tony practically shouts. "We watched him throw you over his shoulder and carry you away."

Scrunching up my nose, I whisper, "It was just a man in a suit." It's not a lie. "Word got out that we were hunters, up here looking for bigfoot, and he thought it would be funny to give us a scare." I hold my breath, hoping they buy it.

"Bullshit!" Brian scoffs. "The way his schlong was wagging, there's no way that was a suit."

My cheeks start to burn red-hot. Oops, I forgot about that part. "I don't know how to explain that, but he changed right in front of me."

Tony slouches down in his seat with a deep frown. I can't tell what he's thinking. Does he believe me, or is he placating me? I hate that I might have planted a seed of doubt into his mind. But if it protects the *sasq'ets*, then I'll do it.

"It's awfully convenient that you come back and suddenly change your story," Darren snorts from the other side of Brian. "At least the bear story was halfway believable."

"Sorry this doesn't fit with your narrative," I clap back at him. "The first time he dumped me in a cave and left. But this last time... he dropped me on the ranger's doorstep and ... revealed himself."

"So that's it?" Darren scoffs. "They don't exist because you got embarrassed by some guy in a ghillie suit."

"Hey, back off, man." Brian jumps to his feet, putting himself between Darren and myself. "Olivia isn't a liar, so if she says it happened like that, then it did."

"Then you're an idiot too." Darren jumps up and stabs his finger in Brian's face. "I didn't come here for this shit. I thought you guys were professionals."

"Dude, what's your problem?" Tony jumps in, stepping up beside Brian. "None of us ever claimed to be *professional*. We came here to camp and *hopefully* find what all of us thought we've seen before."

I appreciate the way these guys are willing to stick up for me, but it's not necessary. Pushing myself to my feet, I place a gentle hand on Tony's shoulder.

"It's fine. I'm used to no one believing I saw what I saw, but I'm not lying." I look past him to Darren. "You can believe whatever you want. No one here is going to stop you from doing that. But me? I think I need a break."

And with that, I turn and make my way across the campsite to my tent. When I push open the mesh door and step inside, my breath catches at the sight of the shredded clothes kicked into the corner from when Sean was here and then shifted.

All of it was true. You're not crazy. It really happened.

Picking up a piece of Sean's shirt, I lift it to my nose and I'm hit with the calming scent of pine after a heavy rain.

Dropping it back to the ground, I look around my normally tidy tent. My sleeping bag is a tangled mess and strewn across the small space. My neatly stacked items are spread all over the floor.

The last words I said to my friends echo through my mind. *I think I need a break.*

And I realize they are true.

Dropping to my knees, I start picking up the scraps of Sean's clothes. Then I move to my bag and sleeping area. For the next hour, I pack up everything inside my tent. When I start to pack that up too, Tony comes over to me.

"Liv?" he says quietly as I push the tent poles into the bag.

When I look up at him, I don't try to hide the tears in my eyes. "Can you give me a ride to my car?"

I'm not sure why I'm so upset over this. It's probably just everything that's happened over the last couple days. And today... today I learned a lot of truths. The kind that make you rethink everything you thought you knew. The kind that you just need to be alone with, so you can get your head straight again.

Tony drops down so he's kneeling in front of me. "Shit, Liv. Did someone—did that guy *hurt* you?"

My heart twists when I realize that he thinks Sean might have— "Oh, no. No, no, no, nothing like that," I assure him.

Tony lets out a relieved breath. "Is it Darren? Please don't feel like you need to leave because of that asshole!"

Leave it to Tony to get me to smile when it's the last thing I feel like doing. "I'm not—it's not—" He drops his chin and cocks an eyebrow at me. I've never been able to get anything past him. "Ok, it's not *all* because of him," I admit.

"What if we ask him to leave?" he suggests, but I'm already shaking my head.

"No. I need some time to think. I've got a lot of things to process." I offer him another smile. "This campsite cost an arm and a leg, so don't waste it. I'll see you at the lodge when the week is up."

Tony helps me finish packing and then we load it all into the SUV. Brian also tries to talk me into staying, but in the end, I think they both understand why I've decided to duck out early.

Darren is, not surprisingly, missing when Tony drives me back down the ridge to where my little hatchback is waiting for me.

CHAPTER FOURTEEN

By the time I make it back up the ridge from town, the sun is low over the horizon, and I've had ample time to think about Olivia. In fact, I can't seem to stop thinking about her. I've replayed every moment with her in my mind. Dwelled on the soft sound of her voice and the even softer press of her lips. I've puzzled over what it is about her sweet scent that makes my squatch lose control. Why I'm so drawn to her.

And I can't come up with a single answer.

I finish unloading all the supplies—including a new door, lock, and two bags of new clothes—before jumping right back in Owen's truck to head back to the campsite.

I need to see her again. I want to talk to her and get to know more about her.

The first stars are dotting the dark blue sky when I pull up to their campfire in a cloud of dust. It's just Brian and Tony sitting by the fire. There is no sign of Olivia.

I greet them with a wave as I come around the front of my truck. "I came to talk with Olivia." I'm scanning the campsite as I ask, but there is something missing. Something I can't quite put my finger on.

"She left," the bearded one, Tony, says from one of the camp chairs. His voice is flat, and he narrows his eyes at me. Accusingly.

My attention recoils like a over stretched rubber band and snaps to him. "What?" Then I realize what's missing. It's her tent. "When? Why?"

Next to Tony, Brian unfolds his long frame from his camp chair and crosses his arms over his chest. "Well, I think we're actually hoping you might be able to tell us."

Oh, great. These guys think I had something to do with her leaving.

And they'd be right, asshole. Leaving without even saying goodbye, especially after the way you kissed her was a dick move.

"Are you the guy?" Tony asks as he stands up beside Brian. I don't miss how his fists are clenched, and he's practically vibrating with anger. "Did you dress up in a suit and carry her off?"

Dress up? For a second, I'm confused as hell at what he's talking about. Then it hits me. Shit...Olivia must have given them a story to explain what happened.

"Er, yeah. I came to apologize. It was... a shitty thing to do."

"Damn right it was!" Brian shouts at me. "Stupid and dangerous! I have half a mind to report you!"

My knee-jerk reaction is to snort at his threat. Even if he did, which I'm a little surprised he hasn't already, the report would go to Owen, and he'd just give me his signature look of disappointment. I hold my hands up, "I know, I know. Look, you have every right to report me, but I really am sorry. I came back to talk to Olivia, to try to make things right. Can you tell me where she went?"

Both men are tight-lipped, and I realize they aren't going to tell me.

"She went back to town. Pretty sure she's staying at the lodge," Darren speaks up from where he suddenly appears on the other side of the fire.

"Darren, shut the fuck up!" Brian hisses at him.

But that's all I need. "Thank you," I holler as I jump back in the truck before any of them can come after me. Then I head back down the mountain, for the second time that day.

I MANAGED to cut the two-ish hour drive back to town down to just over one, and its full dark by the time I pull into the parking lot. I slam Owen's truck into park, not caring that I'm taking up more than one spot.

Rushing into the lobby, I startle the reception girl when I slap my hands on the desk right in front of her. "I need to find out which room a guest is in."

Her eyes spring wide and then they narrow at me. "Really, Sean? You know I can't give out that information."

She's familiar, and I know I've seen her around town. Or maybe we went to school together. My mind spins, trying to remember her name. It's... Sally? No. Sarah? Samantha? Sssss– *Susie!* "Come on, Susie. You know me."

Susie folds her arms across her polo shirt. "And? Are you trying to get me fired?" I give her a pleading look, and she rolls her eyes, "Does she have you listed as an approved contact?"

Shit. "Er, no—how do you know it's a *she*?"

"Because I know your reputation, *Sean Ferrel*." She glares at me. Suddenly, I remember her older sister and I had a thing that ended badly in high school. *Double shit.*

"Look, it's an emergency."

I'm pretty sure she doesn't believe a word I'm saying and narrows her eyes even more.

"Please?" I beg.

She lets out an annoyed sigh, probably realizing I'm not going away until I get this information. "What's her name? I'll ring her room and let her know that you're here to see her."

Relief hits me, and my legs sag. "Thank you! It's Olivia."

She pauses typing and looks up at me. "And her last name?"

Uhhhh. Damnit, I have no idea. "Can't you just use her first name?"

Stepping back from the computer, she reaches over and picks up the phone. Her finger hovers over the number nine. "I think you need to go, or I'm going to call the authorities to make you leave."

Well, I'm just fucking everything up today, aren't I? Stepping back, I hold my hands up. "I'm sorry, Susie. I'll leave. I'm not trying to cause trouble."

She gives me a look that says, *Sure, you're not.* But true to my word, I turn around and leave.

I'm shuffling back to my truck, racking my brain for a way to get in touch with Olivia, when I just happen to look out at the lake and notice a shadow sitting on a park bench. Honestly, if it wasn't for my preternatural eyesight, I never would have noticed them in the first place. Whoever is sitting there could be anyone, but the way my heart picks up in my chest... I have a feeling that maybe... maybe it's her.

Changing course, I jog across the parking lot and then across the grass that's wet with dew and in need of a cut. The closer I get, the more the shape of the shadow starts to resemble Olivia. The way her head is tilted. The color of her hair and how it falls just below her shoulders in a blunt cut. Hope gathers under my ribs just as a gust of wind hits me, and I almost fall to my knees because I'd know that wildflower scent anywhere.

I don't remember the last few steps that take me to her side, but I'll never forget the sadness in her eyes when she looks up at me. My heart twists painfully in my chest. Did I put that there?

My legs give out and I drop to my knees in front of her. "Hey, what's wrong?" I want badly to touch her, but I hold back. For now. It's dark, and I'm not sure if she can see who I am. Or if she wants a man she only met this morning mauling her.

Panic flickers across her face, and she jumps back from me. But then she stops and leans in. "Sean? What are you doing here?"

"I came to apologize," I say before she has a chance to run. "Again."

She stills and cants her head to the side. "Again? For what?" She looks around, squinting into the darkness like she expects someone else. Maybe the guys? But it's just her and me right now.

"For everything," I say, gently resting my hand on the armrest of the bench. The cold dew from the grass is soaking through my pants and into my knees as I gaze up at her. "I'm sorry for carrying you off like I did and then leaving you for my brother to rescue."

"Why did you do that?" she asks softly. "Why did you always leave me?"

My shame leaves a bitter taste in my mouth as I admit, "I couldn't control my squatch, and... I couldn't let you see me in both my forms."

She nods and then turns thoughtful. "And what's different now?"

I stare up at her as I consider her question. "I don't know. It feels right that you know my secret, though."

The corners of her plump lips twitch, but she holds back her smile. "Why didn't you say goodbye when you left me at the campsite this morning?"

I clench my teeth. Do I tell her the truth? Admit that I wanted to snatch her away from her friends and take her back to my cabin to finish what we started at the trailhead? That seeing her with those men nearly sent me into a jealous rage? How can I be honest with her without sounding like a stalker?

In the end, I only shake my head. "I should have; I've felt guilty about it all damn day. You've been all I've thought about since then."

"Well, I didn't say goodbye either," she says with a soft sigh. "So I guess we're even."

It doesn't feel like we're even though. "I stopped by your campsite, and they told me you left. Did I–did you leave because of what I did?"

She does a rapid-fire blink and then shakes her head. "No. *Yes*. It's... complicated."

I lean in, so we're eye to eye. "I'm not usually a complicated guy. Is there a way I can make this right with us?"

"With... *us?*" her voice goes high-pitched and squeaky at the end. It's adorable, and I can't hold back my smile.

"Yeah. I feel like after what happened this morning, we have some unfinished business." I move my hand so it's resting on her thigh. When she doesn't pull away, my next breath comes a little easier. "You left your camping trip early because of me. Right now, you're sad because of me. Telling you 'I'm sorry' seems woefully inadequate. I want to fix this—whatever *this thing* is between us."

A heavy silence stretches as she stares at me. Her brown eyes search mine as she takes in everything I just said. I'm starting to worry that she won't respond at all, when the corner of her mouth turns up into a lopsided smile.

"You certainly have a high opinion of yourself if you think all of this is because of you." When the tip of her little pink tongue darts out to wet her bottom lip, I imagine dipping down and capturing it with my lips, before sucking it into my mouth. I grit my teeth and swallow down a moan when she teases, "And what *thing* do you think there is between us?"

Relief drains out of me like sand through a sieve, and I stand up. Leaning over her, I brace one hand behind her on the back of the bench.

"Tell me if I'm wrong, you feel this chemistry that keeps drawing us together, too." I lean closer, until our noses are almost touching. I gently pinch the tip of her chin between my fingers and tip her head back so she can't look away from me. "And I'm still waiting for you to accept my apology."

The moonlight overhead hits her eyes, turning them silver as she sucks in a sharp breath before whispering, "Accepted."

A growl rumbles up my throat, *"Good girl."* I slam my lips down onto hers, swallowing her whimper. Fuck! Her lips are pillowy soft, and I savor the sweetness of her breath as it mingles with mine. Her eyes flutter closed as she leans forward, she kisses me back.

I'm lost.

My fingers glide across her jaw and then under her hair, curling around the back of her neck. I tease my tongue across the seam of her lips. She opens for me, and I delve inside the heat of her mouth.

Fuck, she tastes just as sweet as I remember. Like warm honey and sweet cream.

Her soft little tongue meets mine eagerly, and her hands clutch the front of my shirt. I prop my knee on the bench beside her, slanting my mouth against hers as I press her back into the bench and show her how I want to fuck her.

Whoa, buddy. Calm down. We haven't even had a first date yet.

We're both breathing heavily when I pull back, but I'm not ready to let her go yet. She's got me primed, and judging by the way she's panting for air, I think she feels the same way.

"I know we barely know each other but..." I growl. "*I want more.*"

Her eyes flutter as she nods. "Me too."

I pull back because... she can't really mean it. But she's looking at me with love-drunk eyes. Her lips are plump from my mouth, and her cheeks are flushed and pink. *Fuck, I bet she's flushed everywhere...*

"Sweetheart, I'm no stranger to no-strings hook-ups," I admit. Except that's not what I want with her. She's nothing like the other women I've had. "But I don't want a one-night stand with you. I want..." *So much more.*

"What do you want?" she whispers. Her fingers tighten in my shirt, and she pulls me down so our noses are nearly touching.

"Olivia," her name comes out a harsh rasp. "I want a whole lot more than your mouth."

Her eyes darken as her pupils expand to eat up all but a sliver of her amber irises. A shudder runs through her as she admits, "This is definitely moving fast, but... Sean, I want you, too."

I groan. Fuck, how can she be so perfect? I have to be imagining this.

"You sure about this?" I whisper against her lips before I kiss her again. "I need to hear you say it, baby. I don't want there to be any miscommunication between us."

"I want you, Sean," she says with a shuddery moan.

"I've never... I don't do things like this, but... I know this is crazy, and we hardly know each other, but I really want this. I want you. I want to see where this goes."

"Jesus, baby, you're—you've got me so turned on right now." I'm so twisted up I'm not sure I'll make it back to her room without coming in my pants.

I expect her to laugh. Or maybe push me away. Instead, her lips curl up into the most adorable smile as she fills the cool night air with the rich honey scent of her arousal. "My room is awfully far away…"

It's like she reads my mind, and I press my forehead against hers. My heart is racing a million miles an hour at the thought that she's gonna let me have her. Just like this. Right now.

"Please, Sean, I need you." To prove it, she spreads her legs so I'm standing between them, and she pulls me down so she can roll her hips against me, seeking exactly what I'm offering.

Decision made, I look around for somewhere I can take her where we won't be seen. The bench is right out in the open, but there is a small grove of spruce and pine nearby that acts as a buffer between the lodge and the lake. I grab her hand and pull her off the bench, toward the trees.

When we're deep enough that I'm reasonably sure no one can see us, I push her back to one of the thicker trunks and lower my head to capture her lips again. Her arms circle my neck, her fingers clutching my shoulders as she kisses me back with a hunger that matches my own.

When I slide my palms under her shirt and up her sides, she lets out a throaty moan as she arches against me.

"We gotta be quiet, baby." My head is swirling with her rich scent, infused with the sharper scents of moss and dew.

I'm not expecting it when she sinks her sharp little teeth into my bottom lip, and I pull away with a chuckle as she looks up at me with lust-glazed eyes. I'm lost. When I kiss her again, it's deep and rough and hard. And she meets me every step of the way.

I curl one arm around her waist as I slide my other hand under her t-shirt so I can cup her breast. Her nipple tightens until it's digging into my palm. She's a perfect handful. My hips rock against hers, pressing my hard length into her much softer tummy.

"You're perfect," I say against her lips as I push the thin material of her bra aside so I can pinch and roll her nipple between my fingers. She arches her back and moans into my mouth as she clutches at me, digging her fingers into my thick biceps.

I lean back and push her shirt up to her neck, so I can see her. I'm still cupping her exposed breast, with her tight nipple that's pink and rosy. Begging for my mouth. I lean down so I can suck it between my lips. At the same time, I pull aside the other side of her bra so I can squeeze and pinch that nipple, too.

Her head kicks back and she gives me a deep, throaty moan. "Sean, *omigod!*"

Pulling back, I let go of her nipple with a *pop*, before I move to her other breast. Cupping her soft flesh, I lick and suckle at her until she's panting my name and digging her short little nails into my shoulders.

Her heady arousal is all around me. The scent of her thick honey making my head spin while she writhes against me.

My cock is fighting against the front of my pants even as I'm hit with a wave of guilt. Olivia deserves better than a quick fuck out in the open. Our first time should be nice and slow. She should be spread out in a plush bed with quiet music and candlelight. Where I have all night to tease and pleasure her, making her come a dozen times before finally sinking deep inside her so we can finish together.

Not fucking her up against a tree.

"Olivia," I moan, pulling away from her lips. "Are you sure you want this? We can go...somewhere else..."

She shakes her head. Her eyes are bright, and even in the darkness, I can see how flushed her cheeks are.

"I want you like this. *Wild*." When she reaches up to pull my head back down to her mouth, I don't fight her. My cock is so hard, it hurts, and my balls are drawn up tight, ready to blow at any moment.

"Fuck, baby," I mutter against her lips. "You're making me crazy. I don't think I can—" Shit, this is gonna be fast. I'm already embarrassingly close to coming in my jeans. With a silent promise to give her slow and romantic later, I step back and spin her around so her front is pressed against the tree.

"Hold on, gorgeous," I rasp as I reach around to unfasten her jeans.

She lets out a throaty moan and wiggles her hips as I push the denim down her thighs. An appreciative sound rolls off my tongue at the sight of her perfect heart-shaped ass. Sliding my hands down her sides, I grab her hips and squeeze, loving how thick she is and how she's giving me something to hold on to.

"Goddamn, baby, you're perfect," I whisper as I pull her hips away from the tree.

I reach into my wallet for a condom first, then the front of my pants. It only takes a second to free myself and wrap up, then I'm pressing the head of my cock against her slick folds. Not just slick, she's *drenched*.

"Look how ready you are for me." I slide back and forth through her lips, coating my cock with her cream.

"Sean, please." She digs her fingers into the bark and

spreads her legs as wide as her pants will let her, twisting her chin over her shoulder so she can watch.

Holy fuck. I think this is the woman I'm going to marry.

I place a soft kiss to the back of her shoulder. "Say that again."

Her breath hitches, and then she meets my eyes and holds them. "*Sean,* I need you."

I can't hold back any longer. Gritting my teeth, I growl her name as I thrust, driving my cock past her lips and into the tight grip of her perfect pussy.

OLIVIA

CHAPTER FIFTEEN

I make the most desperate sound as Sean slides into my body from behind. He's long, and perfectly thick, filling me up and hitting places no one has ever reached before. Dear god, I'm already dangerously close to coming and we haven't even gotten started.

"Fuck, baby, you're so tight," he whispers against my ear. "You okay so far?"

Am I okay? I let out a whimper, because this guy is barely inside me and has already ruined me for any other man. "Don't stop—you feel so good."

He presses another soft kiss against my shoulder, sending shivers down my spine that tighten my nipples because, *holy shit*, who knew shoulder kisses could be so sexy?

Shifting behind me, he pulls back and then presses forward again. My eyes roll back, and my legs threaten to give out. Maybe stand-up tree sex wasn't the best idea, but it's too late now. I dig my fingers into the bark and roll my hips back to meet his next thrust.

"Mmm, that's it, baby. Fuck me back. Show me how you like it."

His dirty talk and sweet shoulder kisses has my pussy clenching around him. I'm willing to bet he's going to make me come first, too.

As we move together, our bodies are perfectly in sync. It's not like the fumbling first-time sex I usually have with a partner. I'm used to taking time to learn their body and how they like to move, but there is none of that with Sean. He seems to instinctively know what I like. And everything I'm doing is working for him too.

He sets an easy rhythm, rolling his hips with each thrust. Slowly building up my orgasm. It's perfect. Until it's not enough. And then, without having to tell him, he reaches around me to slide his hand over my stomach and down…

My breath catches, and I tense when his fingers slide through the patch of soft curls just above my sex before he slips them between my lips. When he brushes lightly across my clit, I jump. Instead of shying away, he whispers dirty things in my ear. His teeth tease my earlobe, and he circles my tight little pearl.

"Sean," I moan. His hips are slapping against my ass as his fingers alternate light flutters with slow slides. "I'm… I can't… *Ohhh!*"

"That's it, baby. Let go, let me feel you."

I'm hanging on to the tree for dear life as my pussy pulses around him and I start to come. My mouth falls open, and a breathy moan works its way up my throat while he rocks in and out of me.

"You're too fucking perfect," he breathes against my ear, holding me tight when my legs turn to jelly. He softly strokes my sensitive clit as I arch and shudder in his arms. "That's it, Olivia. You feel so good… come for me, baby. Come on my cock."

When my orgasm begins to slow he presses his lips to my temple. "One more," he says.

"I can't—" I try to argue, but he pinches my clit between his fingers and sends another orgasm crashing through me on the heels of the first.

"Oh...god!" I gasp as he starts pounding into me from behind. Faster and faster...until he loses his rhythm. He lets out a harsh groan, the sound sends chills racing across my skin. Then his hips roll once...twice. He presses deep and holds.

"*Ahh*." His cock swells and starts to pulse as he moans into the space between my neck and shoulder. "Fuck. *Fuck!*" he grunts each time his cock kicks inside me as he fills the condom with lash after scalding lash of his cum.

When the last ripples of my orgasm slowly evaporate, Sean is supporting most of my weight, since my legs have gone limp-noodle, and his forehead is resting on the back of my neck. He's still filling every inch of me like he's ready for round two, but I'm gonna need some time to recover.

Neither of us moves until our breaths even out and the sweat has cooled on our skin. He pulls back with a soft sigh, and I whimper at the loss of him.

"Are you okay?" he whispers as he pulls my pants and panties back up over my ass.

"Yeah." My heart kicks against my ribs, and a stupid smile spreads across my sex-plumped lips. I've never done it out in the open like this. Where anyone might see. I should feel embarrassed, but I loved it.

When my clothes are set right again, I slowly turn around —disappointed to see that he's redressed as well, and I never got a look at him. Tilting my head back, I meet his heavy-lidded gaze. The way he's staring at me sends shivers running down my spine, and I reach up to place my hand on his chest.

"So, uh, is it a little backward to invite you to come back to my room with me?"

His eyes flash—like, for real. As if a light flickered from inside his pupil. "I was hoping you'd ask." He reaches for my hand and pulls me away from the tree.

When we stride through the lobby of the lodge, he turns to smirk at the shocked look on the hostess's face as we pass, and I make a mental note to ask what *that* is all about.

As soon as the elevator doors open, he rushes me inside and crowds me against the wall. He presses his body against mine and dips his head to capture my lips in a scorching kiss. He nips at the corner of my mouth... strokes my tongue with his... then the doors are opening again.

Now it's my turn to take over. Still gripping his hand, I pull him down the hallway to my room. As soon as the card reader turns green, Sean sweeps me inside, and his lips are on mine again before the door latches shut behind us.

His tongue strokes and slides against mine as he walks me backward, until the backs of my legs hit the bed, and then... Everything happens fast after that.

He's everywhere; and then we're both naked. My hands are pale against his tanned skin as I press them to his chiseled chest. His skin is warm and supple, and I can feel the faint thrum of his heartbeat against my fingertips.

I push him onto the bed and Sean falls back without argument. When I have him spread out before me, I take my time to look. Because this man is *perfection*!

Under the bright lights of my room, I realize his hair is the same color as his squatch's fur: light brown woven with reds and blonds. He keeps it a little longer than his brother's, and right now, its unruliness is giving him a sexy tousled look.

Biting my bottom lip, I drag my eyes down his body, over his bare chest with the smattering of golden-brown hair across his pecs. Then down his washboard abs to the twin cuts of muscle carved into his hips. And lower.

I swallow.

His cock is thick and uncut with a plump purple head peeking through the top of his foreskin. Underneath, a heavy set of balls rests between his thickly muscled thighs.

When I lick my lips, his cock jumps. And that's all the invitation I need.

I crawl between his spread legs and drag my tongue up his shaft before swirling it around his head. Lifting my eyes to meet his, I hum as I lick away the salty drops of cum still clinging to his flesh from earlier.

"Olivia...*goddamn*," he breathes, sinking his fingers into my hair as he watches me.

"You like?" I look up at him, then nip at the soft skin just under his head.

"You're going to make me embarrass myself." His moan turns to a hissed curse when I wrap my fingers around his shaft, lifting him so I can close my lips around his spongy head.

Keeping my eyes on him, I slowly slide my mouth down, down, down until he hits the back of my throat. I hum at the choked sound he makes when I stroke the flat of my tongue along the underside of his shaft.

Before I can drag my lips back up to his crown, and faster than I can process, he bolts upright and flips me so my back is pressed to the mattress and I'm blinking up at him.

"My turn," he rasps as he hitches my legs over his shoulders.

"But–!" I gasp when he dives between my legs, and the heat of his mouth covers my pussy. We both moan loudly when he licks up my center.

Holy shit, I thought he was a master with his dick. But

that's nothing compared to how talented he is with his tongue.

Sean licks me like ice cream, dragging his tongue through my folds and making sure to get every drop of my cream. When he circles my clit with the tip of his tongue, I snap my knees around his head. That doesn't stop him from alternating flicks and soft laps through my sensitive flesh.

"Sean!" With a cry, I arch and buck against his face until he clamps his hands around my hips to hold me still. In hardly any time at all, he has me howling out my pleasure with his head trapped between my thighs.

Licking my slick pleasure from his lips, he wiggles his way free, then crawls up my body and claims my lips once more. Kissing him while tasting myself is a surprising turn-on. Before I can do more than wonder what other turn-on's I might discover with this man, he slides between my spread legs and sinks deep inside me.

"Shit!" he hisses. His eyes go wide and he stiffens, going completely still on top of me.

"What? What's wrong?" My eyes blink open, and I look down at him. Did I do something?

He looks up at me with a sheepish expression. "I forgot a condom."

I've never had sex with someone bare, but having Sean like this doesn't frighten me like it normally would. *Like it probably should.*

His conflict if he should pull out is clear on his face. "I'm clean, I swear."

"I am too," I assure him, "and I'm on birth control."

Sean drops his forehead to mine and whispers, "I've never done this."

"Me either." I cup the sides of his face, gently swiping my thumbs across the smooth texture of his cheeks. When my lips press to his, his cock kicks hard inside me, swelling even bigger.

His tongue plunges past my lips as he pumps his hips to the same rhythm, fucking me into the mattress.

He doesn't stop until he gives me two more orgasms.

I WAKE with the first rays of light filtering through the gauzy curtains.

Damnit, I forgot to close the blackout blinds last night.

You didn't forget. You were distracted, I think as everything from last night comes rushing back: Sean finding me on the park bench. Fucking me against the tree and then coming back here to rock my world for the rest of the night.

I'm half on my stomach, half on my side, with Sean's warmth covering my back. We couldn't have fallen asleep that long ago. Why am I awake now?

As if to answer, the phone beside my bed rings.

I don't remember asking for a wakeup call…

Stretching my arm across the bed, I pick up the handset. "Hhh'lo?" Shit, my voice sounds like I was screaming all night. *Ooops! Because I was.*

"Miss Andersen? This is the front desk. I'm sorry to wake you at such an early hour, but there is a Mr. Darren Jordan here, and he is insisting that he must speak with you. He says it's an emergency."

It takes a minute for my brain to catch up. Darren Jordan? Like… Darren from our group? Is that his last name? *Focus, Liv.*

"An emergency?" I ask—actually it's more of a mumble.

"Yes, miss. He's quite adamant that he speak with you."

"Ummm." I rub at my eyes as I roll out from under Sean. He lets out a groan and then burrows into the warm spot I left as I drag myself so I'm sitting on the edge of the bed.

"Miss Andersen?" the woman on the other end asks.

Suddenly, her message clicks. Darren is here to talk to me about an emergency. Oh, no! What if something happened to Tony or Brian?! "Right. Let me—tell him I'll be right down and to wait in the lobby."

"Thank you, miss. Sorry to disturb you."

I mumble a distracted 'it's fine' and then hang up the phone. By then, Sean is sitting with his back to the headboard, running a hand through his thoroughly disheveled bedhead. *Naw, that's fuck-me hair, and it's sexy as hell!*

"Is everything okay?"

"I'm not sure," I admit with a frown. "Darren is here to talk to me. He says it's an emergency."

Without any hesitation, Sean rolls off the bed and starts gathering up his clothes. So, I do the same, running to the bathroom for a quick shower before pulling on some jeans and a blue t-shirt. This one says *MOIST* in bright yellow bubble letters across my boobs.

I watch with jealousy as Sean runs his fingers through his hair, and the strands magically fall into place. When I do the same, it doesn't have quite the same effect, but this is an emergency, not an interview.

I shove my feet into my shoes and then glance over to see Sean is following me toward the door. "You don't have to—"

He shakes his head. "I don't think you should be alone with him."

"I mean, it's the lobby, so it's technically a public place..."

Sean steps up to me and cups the side of my face with

his large palm. "Baby, I'm not letting you go down there by yourself. I'm not going to be nosy about it, but I'm going to be standing where he can see me."

My heart swells in my chest that Sean would have my back like that. Even Tony and Brian, my friends that I've known for *years*, never made me feel protected the way he does.

I think I love this guy. It's on the tip of my tongue to admit out loud, but I bite it back because... I still hardly know him. You can't love a person after just a day... or even a couple of days. Right?

As we leave my room, Sean slips his hand into mine, and I tighten my fingers around his as we take the elevator down to the lobby. I recall the lust-filled tension that filled the small box the last time we were in it together and how today's tension is much different.

This time, my stomach is roiling with nerves. Something about Darren has always felt a little off to me. I thought maybe I just needed to get to know him, but now I think my inner voice was trying to warn me about him. The closer we get to the lobby, the more nervous I become, and the more relieved I am that Sean insisted on coming. Just before the elevator doors open, I look up at him, nervously.

"I'll be right here," he promises, pulling me against his chest. I take a deep breath and let his comforting woodsy smell soothe some of my worry, while his warmth melts away my anxiety. For a moment, at least. Then the doors slide open, and my nervousness comes rushing back.

"I'll be right behind you," he whispers against my temple as we step out. "If, at any time, you need an out, just make a fist behind your back, and I'll be right there."

Letting out the breath I didn't realize I was holding, I let go and walk past him into the lobby, where Darren is standing in front of the fireplace. His arms are folded across his chest, and his golden hair is a mess. I clear my throat, and he spins around to face me, with blue eyes that are red-rimmed and wild.

Dread tightens my stomach, and I almost curl my arm behind my back and close my fist, signaling to Sean to come intervene, but I hold off.

"Hi, Darren." I hope my smile doesn't look as forced as it feels when I stop, making sure to put a wingback chair between us. "What's going on?"

He drags his bloodshot eyes over me, and I have to fight the urge to brush away the slimy feel of it. Then his face melts into a frightening sneer. "You think you're so smart?"

I reel back. "What are you talking about?" My heart starts to pound and I curl my fingers around the back of the chair.

"Your whole *'bigfoot is just a guy in a suit'* story. You might have fooled the others, but not me. I saw right through your bullshit."

My blood turns to ice as he mocks me. "I—no, that's not—"

"I knew something wasn't right when he came out of your tent. So I followed you. After he left you at that house, I got *this*..." He holds out his phone, practically shoving it in my face, and I have to squint in order to make out what's playing on the small screen. It's a short vid with a bigfoot walking through some trees. Except when he passes behind a thicker trunk, a naked man comes out the other side.

Oh, no.

"Where do they live?" He demands as he pulls the phone back and swipes across the screen. "Where can I find them?"

I'm still trying to process the clip he just showed me as he switches subjects. "What? How should I know?"

"Wrong answer!" he sneers at me. "Tell me where they

are, or I will drag your name through every tabloid and social media site. I'll turn you into a laughingstock so massive, there will be memes around for your kids to see."

I'm trying to keep up while my mind reels. Can he do that? Would he really? "That clip proves nothing," I reply curtly.

"Oh?" He swipes across the screen again and then shows me a grainy photo. This shows Sean's squatch carrying me through the forest . My fingers are tangled in his long fur as I gaze up at him with soft eyes.

Well, shit.

I reach over the chair and swipe at his phone, but Darren holds it up and out of my reach before I can grab it.

"Ah-ah-ah," he taunts me. But then a longer arm reaches over him and plucks his phone out of his hand. "Hey!"

Sean dances back when Darren comes at him, but he's able to easily hold it out of his reach as he starts going through the clips.

"What are you doing! Give that back!" Darren howls.

"I will as soon as I delete these," he says

Darren folds his arms across his chest and taunts him, "Go ahead, I've got them all saved in the cloud."

Without looking up from the screen, Sean smiles. "That's cool. I'm marking them all as AI first, so no one will believe this is an actual clip." When he finishes, he gives Darren a smug look. "So, who's going to be the laughingstock of the internet now?"

With a strangled cry, Darren throws himself at Sean. I barely jump out of the way before they crash together. Sean's back hardly hits the ground before he flips the leaner man over with some kind of MMA move that puts him on his back and in a chokehold.

"What is going on here?" an elderly man wearing the lodge uniform shouts as he jogs over to us.

Sean seems to have things well under control, with his legs and an arm wrapped around Darren, holding him immobile.

"I'm going to have to ask the both of you to leave," the gentleman says pointedly at Darren. "And to kindly not come back."

"I have a reservation—" Darren's argument is cut off—along with his air—when Sean tightens his hold.

"Not anymore, you don't," the older man announces. "Out! Both of you, or I'll call the police."

Sean doesn't seem worried about the threat, but Darren's face is turning redder by the minute. Although that might be from Sean choking him.

Sean finally releases his hold and easily bounces back to his feet. Reaching down, he offers Darren a hand, which he slaps away with a string of curses. Then he snatches his phone that Sean holds out for him.

"You're not going to get away with this," Darren shouts before stalking out the front doors.

"I think we should probably go too," Sean says as he offers the hotel host a charming grin. "We need to warn Owen about him."

"Oh, yeah. You should probably—" I start automatically and then pause when I realize he didn't say *I* but *we*. "I mean, I'm pretty sure that guy kicked you out too." I glance behind him where the older gentleman is back at his desk. He lifts up the phone's handset and points it at us, reminding us of his threat to call the police.

With a big grin, Sean waves at him and then grabs my hand and pulls me out of the lobby.

OLIVIA

CHAPTER SIXTEEN

Owen is waiting for us when we pull up to his house. Leaning his forearms on the banister of the porch, he slowly shakes his head when Sean climbs out of the truck.

"Thanks for finally bringing my truck back, asshole!" he calls out as Sean comes around to help me down from the passenger side.

"Uh, sorry about that."

"No, you're not. Did you even put gas in it like I asked?" When Sean hangs his head, Owen looks to the sky and mutters a string of curses. When he turns his attention to me, his severe expression melts into a tight smile. "It's nice to see you again, Olivia."

"Hi, Owen. Sorry for bothering you so early in the morning."

He chuckles and elbow-checks his younger brother when he comes up the steps. "Like he cares what time it is. Come on then; I've got a pot of coffee brewing."

Not only does he have coffee, but the man has a full breakfast spread waiting for us.

"I think maybe I'm with the wrong brother," I say around an egg and bacon sandwich I made with a bagel.

Sean gives me a mock hurt look before waggling his eyebrows. "Trust me, he can't give you what I can."

"Stop! Right. There," Owen growls, covering his ears. "I don't want to hear another word about what you two are up to on your own time."

My head tilts back with a cackle. I always wished my parents could have had another child, giving me a sibling to tease and fight with. Which means, I'm enjoying the banter between Owen and Sean a little more than I maybe should.

After we've eaten, with refills of coffee, Owen sits down across from us and folds his arms on top of the table. "Okay. So, tell me what happened at the lodge."

I look over at Sean, but he nods for me to tell it. So, I take a deep breath and give him the play-by-play of my encounter with Darren and his attempted blackmail.

Owen is a quiet listener, only speaking up to ask for clarification while I tell my story. When I finish, he's quiet for a bit longer while he mulls it all over.

Slowly, he turns his head to Sean. "The footage?"

"Genuine but easily dismissed. My squatch walks past a tree, and I come out the other side."

"Except for the photo he showed me of your squatch carrying me," I add. "That won't be as easily dismissed."

Sean shakes his head. "Most people can't tell AI from the real thing anymore. There might be some speculation, but most will dismiss it pretty quickly."

Owen's shoulders relax a bit. "That's good. Most people don't believe even the most obvious images, anyway. Hell, people are still arguing over the footage those guys in California took of ol' Wilmer."

Sean sniggers, but I sit up straighter. "Wait. The famous

footage of Bigfoot walking across the rocky river bed *is real*?!"

"Yeah, it's real," Owen admits. "A lot of the so-called proof is real. It's just that no one believes it, so it's easy to explain away. Especially with all the AI garbage that's out there now."

So that's why Sean flagged the footage.

"Researchers think that's a female big—uh, sasquatch. But you said his name is Wilmer?"

"That's right." Sean takes a sip of his mug. "There are no female squatches."

My head swings between the brothers as Owen nods his agreement. "But... how does that work?"

"Well, when a daddy squatch loves a mommy human very much..." Sean can't even finish without dissolving into a fit of giggles.

I shove his shoulder. "Stop! I'm being serious."

"That's kind of how it works," Owen says, grinning into his coffee mug. "Our default setting is human, which is why no one will ever find sasquatch bones. Even if we die as a squatch, we'll automatically return to our human shape. The *sasq'ets* gene is only carried through the paternal line."

"So, you can only have male children?" I ask.

Sean shakes his head. "No, of course not. But any female children won't carry the gene, so they won't shift or pass it to their offspring. Male children usually will though. But not always. It's why we're cautioned to choose our partners wisely."

I'm quiet for a long time as I let this sink in. Particularly the part about choosing a partner. It would make sense to be careful of who you trust with such a wild secret.

Could I be that woman?

Do I want to be?

I watch Sean and Owen talk animatedly across from

each other, and I realize I'm comfortable with him in a way I've never felt with anyone besides my parents. It makes me think it could be easy to fall for him, but how would that work? I live on the other side of the country, and I only have a couple more days before I have to return home.

I've heard so many disastrous stories of failed long-distance relationships. What if it doesn't work between us? Is it worth it to even try?

Sean must feel my eyes on him. He suddenly turns to me and my heart leaps in my chest when his whole face brightens with his smile. Then he reaches for my hand and places a soft kiss to my knuckles, making me want to melt into a puddle.

Yeah, I think I'd be willing to give it a try—if he was willing.

"I'll call Clive and tell him what's going on." Owen turns to me, "Clive is a Salish elder. His family has been keeping our secret since before there were records." Then he turns back to Sean. "He's going to want to meet her."

"Yeah, I figured," Sean replies.

Owen pushes himself back from the table. "You both look like you haven't slept. I'll let you know when he's available to see us. In the meantime," he looks pointedly at me, "I have a guest room you're welcome to crash in."

Before I have a chance to thank him, Sean is on his feet and pulling me up from my chair. "Actually, I think we'll head back to my place to wait. I mean," he gives me a sheepish look, "if that sounds alright with you."

Warmth blooms low in my stomach with anticipation. My words are lost on a soft exhale as I nod.

Sean's much larger hand engulfs mine and he pulls me through the house and out the door. We're across the porch when I turn back to give Owen a wave. "Thank you for breakfast."

I don't have a chance to hear his reply before Sean scoops me up in his arms and runs for the truck. In the distance, I hear Owen shouting after him.

"Don't you dare take my truck again—!" But Sean's already closing me inside the cab and jumping into the driver seat.

It's a short drive down the ridge to his place, but that doesn't stop Sean from grabbing the inside of my thigh and pulling me so I'm sitting right next to him, so close that everything from our shoulders to knees are touching. As the truck bumps along the dirt road, he slides his hand higher... and higher... until his pinkie finger is teasing at the seam of my jeans and I'm squirming at his touch.

Which means it's only fair when I reach over so I can cup his bulge, giving him a squeeze that makes him moan.

"Fuck, baby, if you keep that up, I'm going to drive us into a tree."

I keep teasing him, until he moves his hand to cup my pussy and circles his thumb over my clit, making me moan.

The truck skids to a stop in front of Sean's house. This is my first time seeing it in the daylight. It's maybe half the size of Owen's, but from the outside, it looks almost identical. Right down to the same brown color.

Before I'm able to really admire it, Sean drags me across the driver's seat and sweeps me into his arms, then carries me up the steps. He pauses at the door, that is partly open and hanging askew on its hinges, before nudging it open with his foot.

The inside is exactly as I remember it, except for a pile of plastic store bags filled with clothes and a brand-new door resting across a sofa. A narrow doorway across the room leads into the kitchen, but before I get more than a glance that way, Sean turns left and heads to the back of the house where his room is. The moment we walk through the doorway, I'm hit with his familiar scent of moss, rain and clean forest air.

"Ignore the mess," he growls as he lays me across his bed, where I sink into the soft memory foam mattress.

He pulls his t-shirt over his head, and everything else in the room vanishes. "What mess?"

My fingers itch to trace his wide shoulders and down his thick pecs. When his stomach flexes, revealing a ripple of abdominals, I press my thighs together. His fingers flick at the button on his jeans, and I whimper.

"Baby, this is gonna be over way too fast if you keep looking at me like that."

I can't help it though. Everything about him is ruggedly beautiful.

Pushing myself up, I spread my legs wide so he can step between them as I reach for him. I slide my hands up his waist and then back down again. His skin is soft and warm under my palms. Brushing his hands away from the front of his pants, I pull the zipper down. Letting out a breathy sigh when I'm greeted with more of his golden skin and a dusting of dark hair. No underwear.

Shifting against the ache that's pulsing between my legs, I pull the worn denim down until his cock bobs free. I wrap my fingers around his hot shaft and look up and meet eyes that are heavy lidded. His chest pumps with each breath while he watches me.

Without looking away, I open my mouth to guide him to my tongue, but he stops me just before I have a chance to taste. "Not this time," he says gently as he peels my hand from his cock and kicks his jeans away so he can lean over me. "Lift your arms."

I do as I'm told, and he pulls my shirt over my head. I can practically feel his dark eyes roam across my exposed skin. Then he reaches around me and flicks the clasp of my bra open with one-handed practiced ease.

Without being asked, I slide the plain white lace down my arms and toss it aside.

"Now, lie back, baby."

I do.

He stands at the edge of his bed and watches me for a moment as he slowly strokes his hand up and down his straining cock. Biting my lip, I tuck one arm behind my head so I can watch him better.

Finally, he reaches for the front of my pants. "Lift your hips. That's my good girl." His rumbled praise sends a rush of heat straight between my legs.

In a single pull, he removes my pants and panties. Then he lifts one of my feet and begins kneading his thumbs into the arch before working up to my toes. When I moan, he smiles and brings my foot to his lips, where he kisses my toes, then the ticklish arch before moving up to my ankle. He runs his hands up my calf, followed by more kisses. He bends my knee and places a kiss there too, then gives me a devilish grin as he slides his hands higher.

Spreading my legs, he leaves kisses all the way up the inside of my thigh. By the time he makes it to my pussy, I'm practically shaking with need. To the point that when the first puff of his warm breath hits my center, I'm surprised I don't come right then. My body clenches tight as he softly strokes his knuckles over the top of my seam before dipping a thick finger inside of me.

"Mmm, so tight and wet for me," he groans, then he bends down to circle his tongue around my aching clit. When he gently draws the tight nub between his lips and sucks, my back arches off the mattress.

He watches me raptly as I scream his name and beg for

more as I come apart beneath him. When I come back to myself, he has one hand braced beside me while his cock pulses in his other hand, dripping hot drops of pre-cum onto my stomach.

Pushing myself up onto my elbows, I lift my head to kiss him, but instead his lips drop to my breasts, and he peppers light kisses across the soft swells. My fingers sink into his hair when he draws an aching nipple into his warm mouth. Then he moves to the other nipple, sucking and teasing as he slides his knee between my legs, opening me up for him.

"Sean," I moan. "Please." I'm ready for him again. Needing him to fill me up.

He lets go of my nipple and drags his lips up my chest, to my throat, and then my mouth, where he captures my lips in a searing kiss. Sliding his tongue deep inside to taste and stroke, until I'm overwhelmed with his smokey taste.

He's still kissing me when he shifts himself between my thighs so he can notch his cock at my entrance.

"Yes, right there," I breathe against his mouth. "Please, I need you so bad."

He groans, and his hips press forward, sliding through my drenched folds. He rocks back and forth like this, teasing me until I'm mindless with need. Until finally, he presses his head against my tight entrance.

"Right there," I moan as he pushes deep, stretching me with inch after delicious inch until we're locked together and panting.

"Olivia," my name is a harsh whisper against the side of my neck, "I'm so fucking close. I don't know if I can—"

"Sean. *Please*, shut up and fuck me."

He lets out a dry chuckle. "As you wish." He pulls back and then slams forward. A sob rips through my throat as he hits a bundle of nerves deep inside that has me seeing stars.

"More," I beg.

He pulls back and then slams deep again. And again. *And again.*

My arms and legs are wrapped around him as I meet each thrust with my own. Breathing his name like a chant. Begging him for more, more, *more*. And then *yes, harder!* Telling him how good he feels. *Please. Just like that. I'm going to come...*

My vision swims just before my body explodes into a million bright embers.

Sean's head falls back, and he shouts my name when he comes, filling me until I'm overflowing before he collapses on top of me. Our hearts are pounding to the same rhythm, and we're breathing each other's air as I wrap my arms around him.

He's solid and heavy on top of me, and, at least in that moment, I don't think I've ever felt so content. My eyes grow heavy, and I'm helpless as sleep drags us both into oblivion.

SEAN

CHAPTER SEVENTEEN

I sleep hard and deep with Olivia wrapped tightly in my arms, until the persistent chime of my sat phone wakes me sometime after noon. It's Owen.

"I'm letting you know that I'm heading to your place, since you stole my truck again. So, this is your warning to shower or do whatever you need to before I get there."

I grunt my reply.

"Also, we have a meeting with Clive later this afternoon."

"Yeah. Okay." Then I hang up before he has a chance to bitch at me about his truck again.

After tossing the phone aside, I curl myself around Olivia once more and groan softly into her ear, "We gotta get up and showered. Owen is on his way."

She whines softly as she cuddles against my chest. Jesus, it's the most adorable thing, the way she burrows into me. Having her like this, all soft and sleepy, makes me want to do things to her that will keep us in my bed for the rest of the day. Maybe the rest of the week. Except Owen will be here in about thirty minutes.

"C'mon, baby." I disentangle myself from her so I'm sitting on the edge of the bed.

She pulls her legs up, rolling into a tight ball, which exposes the delicious curve of her ass, and I can't help myself. I smack the flat of my hand against her soft, fleshy cheek. Not hard, but enough that it makes a loud *smack*.

"Hey!" she shouts, bolting upright and glaring at me. "What was that for?"

After pushing myself to my feet, I reach across the bed for Olivia. "We gotta shower and grab some food before Owen gets here."

She blinks sleepily as she lets me help her to her feet, then follows me into the attached bathroom. It's nothing fancy. A glass shower, sink, and toilet.

I start warming up the water and then usher Olivia in first. As tempted as I am to shower with her, I know the moment I get her soapy body within reach, I won't be able to keep my hands off her.

While she showers, I make us a quick lunch. By the time it's ready, she's finished. We switch, and I shower while she eats.

I'm just finishing my sandwich when Owen pushes my front door open and it falls off its hinges. "I thought you were going to fix this?" When he tries to close the door behind him, it refuses to stay shut.

"I am," I say with my mouth full. I point to the new door and hardware that is still propped against the sofa. "Your clothes are somewhere in that pile too."

Shaking his head, Owen gives up on the door and strides into the kitchen. "You're going to end up with bear problems," he grumbles as he starts opening and closing drawers. "Where do you keep your tools?"

I know he won't rest until my door is fixed. I also know he's right about the bears. I'm lucky one hasn't found its way inside yet. After shoving the rest of my sandwich in my mouth, I get my tool bag that I keep in the back of the pantry. Together, we have the new door hung and the locks replaced in record time.

While we are working, Olivia cleans up the kitchen and starts a load of dishes in the washer. She's wiping off the table when we finish.

"Are you ready to go?" I curl my arm around her waist and pull her into my side.

"Sure, where are we going?" Olivia asks.

"Port Angeles." I barely get the words out when my girl's eyes suddenly light up. "What's that look for?" I laugh.

Her cheeks flush a bright pink, but she shakes her head. "I don't have a look! What are you talking about?" But she's failing miserably at trying to hide her smile.

"Spill it, what about Port Angeles has you all excited?" She bites down on her bottom lip and drops her eyes, like she's embarrassed, it's adorable.

"Um, it's on my list of places to check out while I'm up this way, that's all."

I have a feeling there is more than she's telling me, and my curiosity has me pressing. "And why is that?"

"You can't laugh." She covers her face with her hands, so her words come out muffled.

"I promise," but I'm probably lying.

She peeks at me through her fingers. *"Twilight."* Owen and I both groan loudly, but she keeps talking, "I was actually planning to visit both Port Angeles and Forks before I had to head home, but then... well, everything kind of went sideways."

"I can't believe you're a Twi-hard!" I whine, mostly teasing.

"Shut up! You said you wouldn't laugh!"

"I'm not laughing. I think I'm dying on the inside, though."

"Like you have room to judge, Squatch-boy!"

Owen's head kicks back, and his deep laugh fills the room. "She has a point."

Olivia turns away to hide how embarrassed she is at our teasing, and I don't like it. I'll be the first to admit that I don't love how many tourists those movies have brought to our area, but I do appreciate the money and what it's done for our economy.

"You want to go to the restaurant, right?" I ask her quietly. "The one that's based on the movie? *Bella Italia*."

Olivia perks up. "Yes." Then she narrows her eyes. "How do you know about it? Unless–Aha! You're secretly a Twi-hard too!"

I scoff just as Owen adds, "I've heard they have really good food."

"Have you now?" Olivia's teasing grin lights up her whole face as she looks between my brother and me. Then she grows serious. "I'd really like to go."

Well, shit. The way those five words hit the center of my chest, it looks like I'm going to be taking my girl on a guided tour of Forks and La Push at my next chance.

CLIVE LIVES in a modest bungalow that faces the straits. The salty air has faded the cedar siding to a dingy gray, and his small yard is in desperate need of weeding. With a wheelchair ramp that's been built over his front steps that's in dire straits as well.

Before we're out of the truck, Clive is already at the

front door and waiting for us. I don't recall him being that stooped or leaning on his cane so heavily. Then I wonder how long it's been since I've seen him and realize it's been a few years.

"Hey, Clive," I call out as we get closer.

He smiles and waves. He's wearing a clunky pair of glasses and a plaid button-up shirt with his signature bone and silver jewelry. His white hair is pulled back from his face and twisted into a long braid that falls all the way to his waist.

"Come in, boys," he hollers, holding the door open for us. Then he dips his head to Olivia. "It's a pleasure to meet you, miss."

Despite the neglect on the outside of his house, the inside is neat as a pin as he leads us into a small living room. Letting out a loud groan, he falls back into a recliner and then points to the afghan-covered couch next to him.

"So, you've gotten yourselves caught, huh?" He chuckles. "It's been a while since we've had a scandal like that."

Owen and I exchange a sheepish look as we sit down with Olivia between us.

"I am assuming the boys here have explained things to you?" Clive asks her. Olivia nods, and he leans back in his recliner, giving it a nudge with the toe of his cowboy boot to start rocking. "Alright, my dear, Owen filled me in on what's going on, but why don't you tell me your side of what happened?"

Olivia glances up at me and then over at Owen. Then she turns her attention to Clive.

"Well, sir, I came up here to camp with some friends. There was a last-minute change, and one of our friends invited someone who we didn't know. And he's... well, he's the one who's causing trouble. He recorded Sean changing from a squatch to—to human." Olivia twists her fingers together nervously, "Now he's threatening to release the footage and expose Sean if—if I don't tell him where he can find other squatch."

Clive leans forward and pins her with a frown. "And how did he get this footage?"

Olivia turns a nervous look at me, and I nod, encouraging her to tell him everything. "He had a recording and said it was a bigfoot mating call. When he played it, um, Sean came out of the forest and grabbed me."

"There is no such thing as a bigfoot mating call," I tell her gently. Then to Clive, I say, "He was playing a recording of some kind of digitized animal sound."

Olivia turns to me with a frown. "Wait, but if it wasn't a mating call... then why did you come running out of the trees with a—" Her eyes drop to my crotch.

Clive sits up straighter in his chair, suddenly *very* interested in my answer.

I clear my throat to try to hide my embarrassment. "Ah, well, when I got closer, and I picked up your scent—" I spread my hands in a shrug.

"My scent?" Her cute little nose wrinkles.

I lean forward to whisper so only she can hear me. "You smell really fucking good, baby."

Beside us, Owen clears his throat. "And why don't you tell us what happened next, Sean?"

I'm sure my face turns beet red with even more embarrassment as I finish Olivia's story. Recalling how I kidnapped her and took her to the cave—although I conveniently omit the NSFW parts.

Clive listens patiently until we've finished, then he suddenly bursts into a peal of hearty cackles. "So you're telling me you found yourself a woman who came out here searching for bigfoot?" He leans forward and slaps his knee. "I mean, no one's ever going to believe that."

Beside me, Olivia clenches her fists on her knees, and I reach over to cover one.

"I didn't come *searching* for bigfoot," she bites back as she pushes my hand away. "Just...hoping, I guess. Me and my friends, each one of us had an experience. I saw one when I was a little girl when I wandered away into the woods and got lost. He—led me back to my family."

Clive grows serious. "You know, the *sasq'ets* don't just reveal themselves to anyone."

A smile tugs at the corners of her mouth, and she tilts her head to the side. "Yes, that's what I hear. But what does that mean? There's nothing special about me."

I open my mouth to disagree with her, but Clive leans forward in his chair and levels her with a serious expression. "There are many legends of the *sasq'ets*, but a common theme is that they are known as protectors. They've always watched over the forest and those inhabiting it. So, when you got lost, I suspect you fell into the category of needing protection."

Olivia leans back into the couch cushions with a smile. "That's very sweet. I like that explanation."

"Well," Clive takes off his glasses to wipe at his eyes before settling them back on his nose, "I'll spread the word to the others. Let them know what happened and to watch out for—"

"Darren," Olivia interjects.

"Right. Darren. By tomorrow, I'm sure everyone will know about it, and you know we'll all corroborate your story. Help build you a nice little alibi should you need one. In the meantime..." Clive pushes himself out of his chair with a groan and then crosses the room and opens the door.

"Wait. That's it?" The words are out of my mouth before I can stop them.

"Well, yeah." Clive looks us over for the moment.

"What did you think, you were going to get a blessing for being a dumb shit or something?"

Olivia tries not to laugh, but her shaking shoulders give her away, and a smile spreads across Clive's wide mouth. "Here's some advice for you. Don't fuck it up with that one. I like her."

Owen starts laughing too, and I give them both my fiercest glare.

"And that goes for you too," Clive adds, pointing a gnarled finger at Owen.

"Me?" His eyes grow wide when he points to himself.

"Yes, you. You need to do right by that little lady you've been stringing along. It's long past time you settled down." He sweeps his hand from Owen to the door. "Now, get out. I've got bingo tonight, and my ride will be here any time now."

CHAPTER EIGHTEEN

We're quiet when we leave Clive's house, each of us thinking about what he said. In fact, I'm so far into my thoughts, I forget why we're stopping when Owen pulls into an inconspicuous strip mall.

It's not until Sean opens the door and I see the sign in swooping script.

Bella Italia.

My heart leaps in my chest, and my excitement returns. I'm really going to eat here!

I give up trying to hold back my grin as Sean helps me down from the truck. When my feet hit the ground, he leans down to whisper in my ear, "You'll have to tell me everything you want, so I can keep that look on your face permanently." Then he presses his lips to my temple, and my heart flutters.

We're seated quickly in the back by a window that looks out over the quiet street. Sean and I sit together with Owen across from us as the hostess hands us menus and takes our drink orders. I open the menu and do a cursory glance through it, but I already know what I'm going to order.

A few minutes later, the waitress arrives with our drinks, a Pino gris for me and beer for Sean. Owen opts to stick with water, since he's driving.

"Are we ready to order?" the waitress asks, pulling out a handheld device.

Owen and Sean both turn to look at me.

"Oh. Um, yes. I'd like the—" I feel my cheeks grow hot, "—the mushroom ravioli please."

Her head snaps up, and she looks at me for a moment before her red-painted lips spread into a knowing grin. "Excellent choice." She glances over at Sean and then Owen. "And is this a Team Edward or Jacob situation?"

I turn to Sean, and before I can stop myself, I say, "I guess I'm Team Jacob."

Sean, Owen and the waitress burst out laughing, while I want nothing more than to crawl under the table.

After she's taken the guys' orders, and we're left alone, Owen leans across the table and asks, "What's Team Jacob?"

"Um, so, in the books, Jacob shifts into a giant wolf."

"Better than a glittery bloodsucker." Sean grins down at me and lifts my chin with his finger to kiss my lips.

It's at that moment my cell phone suddenly starts buzzing in my pocket. It's such a habit to carry it around, I always keep it on me, even though I haven't had much service—until now.

Pulling back from Sean, I glance down at the screen and apologize. "It's Tony. I need to take it." I swipe my thumb across the screen as I lift it to my ear. "Hey."

"Oh, thank god!" Tony's voice is all kinds of relieved.

Suddenly, I'm on high alert. "What's wrong?"

"I was worried about you," Tony says, "so I came down to the lodge to check on you, but the front desk said you left early this morning and haven't been back."

"I'm sorry I worried you. I didn't think to leave a note for you or a message on your phone. I've been... out. Doing some sightseeing." I glance up at Sean and shrug. "What's going on? Is everything okay?"

There is a long pause, and I can hear Brian in the background before Tony asks, "Have you heard from Darren, by chance?"

My blood turns cold. "As a matter of fact, I have. Why?"

"He took off last night, and we hadn't seen or heard from him since." And just like that, all my anxiety is back. "You haven't left, have you? You're still coming back to the lodge?"

I glance at Sean again, who nods—because of course he has super hearing and can probably hear the whole conversation. "Yeah, I'll be back later tonight. I'm in Port Angeles right now, having dinner."

"Brian and I are at the lodge. We'll wait for you; we really need to talk." There is another pause, and then Tony asks quietly, "Are you okay? The way you left, I feel awful that I didn't stick up more for you."

"I'm okay, Tony. Thank you, but I'm a big girl, and I can handle myself against bullies."

"Okay, good." I can practically hear the relief in his voice. Then he adds, "Enjoy your mushroom ravioli, and we'll see you when you get back."

"Thanks, I — wait! How did you know?"

"I've known you since we were teenagers. You think I forgot how into those books you were?"

"Nice. Speaking of... my dinner just arrived," I say as I catch sight of the waitress heading our way.

"Okay, I'll see you in a few hours."

I shove my phone back in my pocket just as my dish is placed in front of me. The savory scent of the parmesan and earthy mushrooms has my mouth watering and helps to blot out the stress of my phone call.

"Thank you again for bringing me here," I say to Sean after we're left alone once more.

His dark eyes roam over my face as his lips twist up into a smile. "You're welcome, baby."

The way he calls me baby, like he did when he was inside me, sends heat rushing to my cheeks… and lower. Forcing my attention back to my plate, I scoop up a steaming ravioli and blow across the top before taking a bite. My eyes roll back, and I can't stop my moan as the rich flavor bursts across my tongue.

"I will never get tired of hearing you make that sound," Sean whispers in my ear before he picks up his hamburger and takes a giant bite.

Across the table, Owen is shaking his head and trying to ignore us.

SEAN

CHAPTER NINETEEN

It's well past dark, and much later than we intended, when Owen drops us off at the lodge. He drives off with little more than a wave, leaving me stranded and at Olivia's mercy. Not that I have any complaints. Especially when she slides her hand into mine and smiles, assuring me that she won't be kicking me out of her bed tonight.

We walk toward the lodge, hand in hand, as she calls Tony to let him know we're here.

I can't help listening as Tony fills her in on the latest drama. I don't mean to eavesdrop—or maybe, I do—but it's kind of hard not to when you have preternatural hearing.

Tony and Brian were supposed to camp up on the ridge for one more night, but after Olivia and Darren both split, they packed it all up and came back to the lodge to see if they could get an extra night added to their reservations.

"No way!" Olivia gasps. "There weren't any double occupancy rooms available *at all*?"

"That's what I said," I hear Tony laugh through her phone. "Brian's a great guy and all, but I'm not really into sharing a bed with him. Luckily, they are giving me a roll away so we don't have to snuggle."

"You're going to make Carmen jealous," she teases him, and I decide that maybe I like Tony a little more knowing he has a girlfriend.

"Doubt it," he scoffs. "She reads those *why choose* books. Lord knows what kind of ideas she'd get if she knew I was sleeping with another dude."

"Uh, please keep me out of your fantasies, bro," Brian shouts from the background.

Olivia is laughing so hard, she has to stop in the middle of the parking lot to catch her breath. "Let's not ever discuss that again," she wheezes then glances down at the time. "Oh, shit. I didn't realize it was so late. The restaurant is probably closed by now."

"Oh, yeah, I think it closed an hour ago. We'll just meet for breakfast, okay?"

"Are you sure?" she asks. "It sounded important. Do you want to meet in the lobby or something?"

"Liv, I'm looking out my window at you, and I can see you holding hands with that park ranger. You've been spending a lot of time with him. Are you sure that's wise after what he did?"

Olivia's head tilts back and she scans the windows for which one Tony is watching her from. "When you say it like that, it sounds like... like you don't trust me."

"It's not that," Tony mutters. "I just—I don't like that guy. After what he did to you, it's *him* I don't trust."

The tension running through her hand and into mine relaxes, and she looks up at me with a soft smile. "You know I will always appreciate your honesty. This time... I've gotten to know Sean, and..." She worries her bottom lip between her teeth as she tries to think of how to assure her friend that I'm not the monster he thinks I am. "And I'm finding out he's not at all what I thought."

I can hear Tony's heavy sigh just before he grumbles, "If he breaks your heart, I'm gonna break his legs."

Olivia giggles. "I'll be sure to warn him."

"Yeah, see that you do," he says dryly. Out of the corner of my eye, I catch the flutter of a curtain, just as Tony moves away from the window. "Just... be careful, and we'll see you at breakfast."

When she looks back at me, I can practically feel the heat radiating off her cheeks.

"We'll see you at breakfast then. Good night." My heart starts to pound when she doesn't try to make up an excuse and instead comes right out and admits her intentions are to spend the night with me.

Which means Olivia and I have the rest of the night to ourselves.

My fingers tighten around her smaller hand as I set a quick pace back to the lodge. The moment she lets us into her room, I'm hit with all the erotic memories from the night before. The bedding has been changed and the room tidied, but I can't wait to mess it all up again.

My gaze slides over to where Olivia is kneeling beside her carry-on. When she stands up, she's got a bundle of clothes in her arms. "I'm going to take a shower, if you don't mind."

"No, not at all." I offer her a smile and then watch her slip into the bathroom. A moment later the shower turns on. My gaze lingers on her luggage, and it hits me that the time I have with her is coming to an end.

How am I going to convince her to stay? If she can't, or won't, how am I going to watch her go?

It's a question that's been bouncing around in my head

more and more. I remind myself that I haven't even known her for a week. But the way I feel, it's more than just lust. I can't ignore the way my squatch homed in on her. Or the more time I spend with her, the faster I'm falling for her. Which means it's going to be that much harder to watch her go. Because she will go. Her whole life is across the country, and I haven't earned the right to ask her to uproot everything she's built. It would be no different if she were to ask me to just pack up my whole life and move to a place I've never been.

You could, though. You have people in the mountains there.

I know they exist, but I've never met them. I can't just show up and integrate myself into their territory.

I drag my gaze over to the window that is covered with thick black-out curtains, imagining the landscape on the other side. These mountains are my home. I've never lived anywhere else, and until just now, I've never considered leaving.

The sound of the water changes, and my thoughts shift to Olivia. I imagine her stepping under the spray, naked. Tilting her face back and letting the water cascade down her body, over her breast and down her legs. With my next breath, I'm across the room, curling my fingers around the doorknob. I twist.

It turns easily. She didn't lock it.

Considering that invitation enough, I let myself into the brightly lit room that's heavily fogged with steam. Closing the door softly behind me, I step deeper into the room where the shower is tucked into the corner. It's larger than I expected. Through the fogged glass I can just make out the shape of her as she runs a washcloth up her arms and across her chest.

Taking a step back, I should let her shower in peace, but then she lets out a soft, throaty moan as she drags the soapy cloth across her breasts. My mouth goes dry and I imagine how the rough cloth must feel against her sensitive nipples. They are probably beaded to tight tips, and my mouth waters to taste them again.

She slowly drags it down her stomach and her breath hitches when she dips the cloth lower and lower… until *holy shit*, she sweeps it between her legs.

The way her low moans mingle with the sound of the water has my cock pressing against my zipper, begging me to go in there and help her out. I can't see details through the foggy glass, but I can tell she's leaning back against the tile, with one hand cupping a breast, while the other works the cloth between her legs.

"Mmm," she hums. Her head falls back, showing the long column of her throat. Then suddenly the cloth drops with a splat to the ground, but her fingers are still working between her legs. "Oh, mmm, that's so good." Her breath hitches with a whimper. "*Sean*, please."

The sound of my name as her hips buck against her fingers is all the invitation I need.

I have the presence of mind to toe off my shoes, but that's all as I reach for the glass door and step inside. Fully dressed.

Her eyes snap open, and a breathy giggle floats through the space as she keeps working her fingers back and forth across her clit.

"You're not going to undress?" she asks just before I drop to my knees before her. Gently, I curl my fingers around her wrist and pull her hand away so I can suck the sweet pussy juices from her fingers. "Oh, holy shit, that's hot."

Twirling my tongue, I make sure to get every delicious drop before I slide my hands up her thighs to grip her hips. "Lift your leg for me, baby."

She does, and I drape it over my shoulder, opening her up for me. "Good girl," I rumble, feasting my eyes on her glistening slit. "Now I'm going to clean up this mess you made."

The leg she's standing on threatens to give out, but I've got her. Tipping my chin up, I press my mouth against her dripping center. Licking and nibbling, making sure to taste every inch before turning my attention to her clit. I tease tight circles with the tip of my tongue until her breaths are coming in shallow pants and her fingers are gripping my hair. I build her up and then back away. Edging her until her orgasm crashes into her and my name echoes through the bathroom as she drenches my face with her cum.

Leaning back, I lick her sweet taste from my lips. Her warm brown eyes are heavy-lidded and glazed as I slide her leg from my shoulder and make sure she's got her balance before I pull my soaking shirt over my head, followed by my jeans. I kick them into a soggy pile in the corner before I'm crowding her against the wall.

"Can you take me again?" I ask, reaching up to gently brush my thumb across the smooth skin of her cheek. This close, under the bright lights, I notice a light smattering of freckles across the bridge of her nose, and I add them to the long list of things about her that I'm quickly falling in love with.

Her lips flush a dark pink when she nods.

That's all the consent I need. I grab behind her knees and lift her off her feet so her legs are hitched around my hips. "Touch me. I want to feel your hand wrapped around me," I say, then almost lose it when she reaches between us. Her palm is warm and wet from the shower, and her grip is *perfect* when she wraps her fingers around my thick length. "Just like that. Now. Guide me home, baby."

Olivia rolls her hips as she notches the tip of my cock at her entrance. She's so wet for me that I slide in with ease.

"Sean, you feel so good," she whispers as she circles my neck with her arms. My knees threaten to buckle as she makes the sexiest sounds against my ear.

"So do you, baby." My voice is hoarse as I press her back to the tile, fucking her with long, deep strokes. Her body grips me tight, like we were custom-made for each other. "I swear, every time is like the first time with you."

Olivia digs her nails into my shoulders and hooks her ankles at the small of my back so she can rock her hips in time with my thrusts. "Same—I feel... it's never been this good before."

I capture her lips, slanting my mouth over hers as she meets every stroke and slide of my lips and tongue. I want to drag this out. I want it to last forever. But this woman is too perfect, she destroys my self-control every time I get inside her.

"Sean—" Her breath catches as her pussy tightens around me. It's a tell, I'm learning, that she's close. "Come with me," she begs.

"Always," I whisper against her lips.

Widening my stance, I thrust harder, working myself as deep as I can get. Her head falls back against the tile with a choked sob, and then it happens. My balls draw up tight as her pussy clamps down around me, and we come together. It's something I've never experienced before, and I know I'm going to be addicted to it from now on.

Which means I gotta figure out a way to make her stay.

CHAPTER TWENTY

Sean's sitting with his back to the headboard, his eyes are dark with lust and locked with mine. I have my arms draped over his shoulders, my fingers carding through his silky-soft hair, toying with the short strands at the base of his neck while I roll my hips up and down his cock while he grips my ass. His fingertips dig into my soft flesh, as he sets the pace.

His eyes drop to my chest, where he watches my breasts bounce and sway. Suddenly, a thought comes to me. One that makes my cheeks heat. It's such a naughty thought, and it has my hips rocking faster and harder the more I think of it.

"Hmm, what just happened, baby?" Sean's lips quirk up, and his hands tighten on my hips as he urges me to rock up and down faster. "What are you thinking about that got you so hot all of a sudden?"

I don't really want to tell him, but I can't seem to keep anything from him either.

"I—I was thinking about you," I admit. But that's not exactly what was on my mind.

"Oh yeah? And what did I do that got you so worked up?"

I bite down on my lip. "I was remembering the first time I saw you. When you came crashing through the forest and threw me over your shoulder."

Sean lifts one of his brows, curiously. "Uh-huh. And what else do you remember from that night?"

"I remember watching you stroke yourself." My grip on the back of his neck tightens and I snap my hips up and down his thickness. "I was mesmerized at how big you are."

Sean lets out a grunt and sits up, pressing our chests together as he grinds me down on his cock.

"And I started to wonder," I moan—he's hitting that bundle of nerves that's so deep, the one that makes me forget my name. "Have you ever... fucked as... *him*?"

The room spins, and suddenly I'm flat on my back with my knees almost pressed to my shoulders. Sean braces himself above me as he plunges in and out my tight pussy.

"Would you want that?" he growls down at me. "You want to be fucked by a monster? By my squatch?"

I nod, because—*holy shit, yes. I want that!* Then I cry out when my orgasm suddenly electrifies me.

"Do you want me to stretch your pussy with my giant squatch cock?" His voice is rough, and his words are so filthy.

"Yes! Yes, I want that," I tell him, squeezing my eyes shut as my entire body lights up like the Fourth of July. Anyone in the hallway can probably hear my screams, and I don't give a damn.

"Fuck, baby," is all he says before he pounds in and out of me. He lets out a loud groan, filling me until he's spent.

We don't speak of it again. Not after we quickly shower and dress. Not as we straighten the room. It's not until we're walking down the hall that he leans against me and whispers into my ear, "I've never done that before, but I want that with you. If you really want that with me."

The grin I wear the rest of the way to breakfast could light up the entire West Coast.

Tony and Brian are already waiting for us at a table. I wave as we make our way through the dining room. Brian's face lights up with a grin, when he sees us. But Tony's eyes narrow slightly when he looks down at our linked hands.

"Hey, guys," I say as Sean pulls my chair out for me. "This is Sean."

Tony's expression remains narrowed while Brian reaches across the table to shake his hand. "Nice to finally meet the guy who's snatched up our girl," he jokes.

Sean gives his hand a strong shake and then holds his hand out for Tony. "It's nice to officially meet you."

Tony doesn't move for a moment before he accepts his offered hand, squeezing Sean's fingers hard enough that they blanch white when he lets go. If Sean is bothered by the show of force, he doesn't let on.

"So you guys already know Sean's a park ranger." I'm sure my cheeks are bright red as I remember exactly how I ended up in that cave. "He, ah, he..."

"It was a bad joke to try and scare you guys," Sean interrupts. Then he turns to me. "But I can't say I'm sorry about the outcome."

"A joke?" Tony sputters. "Kidnapping Olivia was a *joke* to you?"

I reach across the table and place my hand over his wrist. "It's fine. He apologized, and I forgave him."

"Well, what about me? Us!" He points beside him at Brian. "This whole week has been one thing after another. This was supposed to be hanging out, hiking and telling ghost stories around the fire, and instead you get carried off and Darren goes AWOL. No offense, Liv, but this camping trip sucks."

My stomach twists, and I fall back into my seat. Fuck. When he puts it like that...

Tears suddenly burn the backs of my eyes. "You're right. You are absolutely right to be pissed. Hell, I'd be pissed. I'm so sorry–"

Tony backpedals when he realizes he's upset me. "Liv, you don't need to be sorry. I'm not trying to heap this on you." he lets out a harsh exhale, "That was unfair of me, because none of this is really your fault either. It's just the way everything keeps happening..."

"Stop it, you two. If anyone should be sorry, it's me," Brian cuts in. "If I hadn't brought Darren, I don't think any of this would have happened."

"But you couldn't have known..." My voice trails off when the waiter comes over to our table with a carafe of fresh coffee.

After our mugs are filled and our orders have been taken, Brian clears his throat and leans over his folded arms, looking me pointedly in the eye. "I had no idea Darren was..." he lifts a hand and shakes his head, "*like this*. But I still shouldn't have invited him the way I did. And I'm even more sorry about not calling him out on the way I caught him watching you."

A cold chill sneaks up my spine. "Wait. He was *watching me*?"

Brian slowly nods. "I thought if I just kept an eye on him, that would be enough to keep you safe."

Sean goes stiff beside me and I reach under the table,

placing my hand on his thigh. Nothing I can do about what's already happened. At least Brian's telling me about it now.

"I wish you would have said something sooner." My head swings back and forth between Brian and Tony. "Have either of you heard from him?"

Both men share a look and then shake their heads.

"He took off shortly after you did," Tony says.

Sean speaks up, leveling them with a narrow look, "You should know that yesterday he came to the lodge looking for Olivia. And then he tried to blackmail her."

"Blackmail?" Brian sits back in his chair. "About what?"

Well, I wasn't planning on bringing *that* up. But since he did... "He thinks he has proof of Sean turning from a bigfoot into a man."

Brian and Tony wear matching puzzled looks as they turn to stare at Sean—who is very much human.

"Wow," Brian slowly shakes his head, "you think you know a guy, then find out that he might actually be crazy."

Relief washes over me like ice water when they don't question the possibility that sasquatch shifters might actually be real. Because why would they? The only reason I believe it is because I saw it with my own eyes. More than once.

A loud crash makes me jump, and every head in the restaurant snaps to where the French doors are flung wide open. Standing in the opening, as if summoned, is Darren. It's late enough in the morning that there are only a few tables occupied, but Darren has made sure he has everyone's attention as he scans the room. When he finds us, his expression turns smug, and he strides toward us with a small entourage following behind him.

"What the hell?" Tony mutters under his breath as Darren marches straight to our table.

"Darren, my dude, what are you doing?" Brian jumps to his feet, trying to intercept him, but Darren's focus is on me as he dodges and then slips past him. His blue eyes are bright and manic, and his pupils are dilated so wide that I wonder if he might be on something.

Beside me, Sean's chair scratches across the hardwood floor as he pushes himself to his feet.

Darren's focus switches from me to Sean, and he points a shaking finger at him. "I know what you are!"

I can't help but feel sorry for him. Even though he's not wrong... behaving this way isn't going to make anyone believe him.

"Darren—" Brian tries again to insert himself between us.

"Don't!" Darren warns him. "I can prove it."

He fumbles with his phone, and Brian gives me a sympathetic look as I shrug. If it's the same footage he showed us, I'm not worried, but if he managed to get something else... My stomach tightens, and I glance nervously at Sean.

The room is deathly quiet as the morning diners watch us raptly. The three men who came in with Darren are standing like hired security, except for the one who has a handheld camera and is recording the entire interaction.

Shoving his cell phone at Brian, Darren can hardly hold still as the video plays, and I wonder how much Brian can actually see. Whatever it is, the look he gives Darren when it ends is sympathetic, and I release the breath I was holding.

"Look, man, let's go somewhere else so we can talk about this, okay?" When Brian reaches out, Darren jumps back.

"What is there to talk about?" he asks loudly, stabbing his finger at his cell phone screen. "You saw it!"

Brian scrunches up his forehead. "I saw *something*," he admits, "but this isn't the place to discuss it. We're ruining these nice people's meals."

Looking around, I see no one truly seems bothered by our theatrics.

Darren stabs a hand into his blond hair, gripping the already wild strands. He shakes his head and mutters something that sounds like, "*I'll make you see.*"

Without any warning, he lunges, grabbing me by the hair and jerking me out of my seat. My startled scream cuts through the quiet and I wrap shaking hands around his wrists as my feet scramble against the wood floor.

"Let me go!" All my attempts to pry his hand from my hair are futile. Darren has several inches and probably sixty pounds on me—add to that his enraged state, and he's able to drag me away from the table with ease.

Sean jumps to his feet, sending his chair toppling over behind him. "Get your hands off her!"

The smell of sweat and greasy fast food wafting off of him makes my eyes water as he pins my back to his chest with one arm. He lifts his other hand up, and my breath stills when I realize he's holding a knife. He presses the sharp steel against my jugular, and I squeeze my eyes shut with a whimper.

All around me, the room has erupted into chaos. Several diners have their cell phones out and the wait staff is watching us anxiously. The hostess has her phone to her ear and is talking quietly, hopefully calling the police.

"Darren, please," my voice is barely a whisper.

"Shut up!" he hisses against the side of my face, making me flinch. "Do it! Show them!" he shouts. But he's not talking to me, he's talking to Sean. "Show them what you are, or I'll slice her throat."

CHAPTER TWENTY-ONE

When Darren lunges for Olivia, I move too, sending my chair skidding out from behind me. I move to charge at him, but he's already pulling her out of my reach. The flash of metal against her neck freezes me in place and sends my heartbeat skyrocketing. It takes every bit of my strength to keep from squatching out.

"Do it! Show them!" Darren shouts at me. His eyes are wild, and I can't look away from where he is carelessly pressing the blade to her throat. If he so much as nicks her perfect skin, I can't guarantee I'll be able to hold on.

Inside my head, my squatch howls his frustration at the danger our girl is in.

Not yet. My control over him has never been this tenuous, but knowing that's exactly what Darren wants gives me the strength to hold him back.

As soon as Darren stormed into the restaurant dining room I had a feeling that something was about to go down. I sent a text to Owen, just before Darren grabbed Olivia. Now, all I can do is hope he'll pass the warning to some of the locals, before all hell breaks loose. All I can do now is keep my cool so Olivia doesn't get hurt while I wait for backup.

Fear has leached all the color from her cheeks, but her eyes are steady and calm, locked with mine as she silently tells me to hold on. Begging me to keep my squatch hidden. Except, there is no telling how long it might take for help to come, and the longer my girl is in danger, the weaker my grip becomes.

"Put the knife down. Olivia hasn't done anything to deserve being treated this way." I hold my hands up, trying to reason with him.

"Yeah, man," the cameraman suddenly speaks up. "I didn't sign up for anyone getting hurt."

"Shut up and keep recording!" Darren hisses at him, then turns his attention back on me. "My brother wasn't doing anything either when the bigfoot came rushing out of the woods at him. We were deer hunting, and then suddenly he just came out of nowhere. Of course, no one believed me. They thought I killed Johnny. They sent me to *jail,* but I'll finally be able to prove that it wasn't me."

The cameraman glances over at the other two, who shrug, and he holds the camera up again.

Turning his attention back to me, Darren presses the knife harder against Olivia's throat. "Do it! Now!"

"Do what?" I shout back at him trying and failing to keep the panic I'm feeling out of my voice. "I can't do what you expect me to do!"

"Quit playing dumb. Turn into bigfoot like I saw you." He glances at Olivia. "Or, I swear, I'll hurt her until you do!"

Olivia lets out a soft whimper, even as she shakes her head, just slightly. Pleading for me not to do it.

The tense silence stretches, and Darren slowly drags the sharp tip up and down the side of her neck. "Fine. I warned you." He turns so his lips are pressed to the shell of her ear. "For what it's worth, I'm sorry, Liv."

She squeezes her eyes shut when he presses the knife's edge deeper against the side of her throat, and the familiar tingle of my shift starts in my fingertips. Just then, the sound of sirens and tires skidding on blacktop come from outside. Icy relief washes over me, and I curl my hands around the sharp claws that have broken through the ends of my fingers.

"What is going on here?" a voice booms just before a tall man in a police uniform storms into the restaurant. The moment he sees the weapon in Darren's hand, the officer draws his taser. "Drop the knife."

Several more cops file into the dining room behind him, followed by a small group of elders I recognize from nearby tribes. Seeing them helps me relax enough that the tingling in my fingers subsides.

"Keep recording, Alex," Darren barks at the cameraman. "I'll show everyone!"

But Alex and the other two are already backing away with their hands up as the police pull them aside.

When Darren realizes his stunt isn't going to work in his favor, he turns to run. Olivia is still pressed to his chest when the officer fires his taser. The prongs dig into his back, sending 90,000 volts through his body. With a strangled sound, he stiffens like a board and the knife falls from his fingers.

Unharmed, Olivia pulls herself away from him and runs right into my arms.

"Oh, my God!" she sobs against my chest.

"It's alright, baby. I've got you. You're alright now." I'm probably holding her too tight, but I can't loosen my arms. I need to feel her heartbeat pounding against mine and hear each shuttered breath, so I know she's safe.

When her pulse has calmed a bit, she looks up at me with brown eyes that are wide and worried. "I thought—I was so scared that you might..." She glances around and then presses her face back into my chest.

My arms tighten around her. Leave it to this woman to worry about me, when she was the one in danger.

"That was never going to happen," I lie, because it was close. Too close.

Her head snaps up again, and this time she is glaring at me. "I saw your hands, you idiot!" she hisses at me, then pinches my side. *Hard.* "You sprouted claws."

I can't help laughing as I pull her back against my chest. "It's okay. No one noticed."

She scoffs. "If I noticed your hands, then it's probably on someone's recording," she whispers into my chest.

I glance over my shoulder and see a couple of the elders with the cameraman. One has his camera, and I suspect any footage will be erased when he gives it back.

The officers have Darren cuffed and are dragging him out of the restaurant when Owen comes rushing through the doors. His eyes are worried as he looks around. When he finds me, his whole body sags with relief, and he pushes through the mingling cops to get to me.

"I called for help as soon as I got your message and then got here as fast as I could." He's out of breath, and his eyes are looking everywhere at once, taking in the aftermath. "What the hell happened?"

It's been less than an hour since I messaged him, and it takes twice that to drive down from the mountain. "How did you get here so fast?"

"I was already in town." Over his shoulder, I notice Jenny from the general store standing quietly against the back wall, taking everything in. She's wearing jeans and a black t-shirt with a red and black flannel tied around her waist. Her black hair is pulled up into a high ponytail, and her arms are decorated with colorful full-sleeve tattoos.

Wait, does this mean he was with Jenny last night? How often does he do this?

"Is there something you'd like to talk to me about?" I ask when Jenny pushes off the wall and comes over to join us.

"Nope," Owen tells me before he turns to the woman. "Jen? You've met my brother, Sean." She smiles and nods. "And this is Olivia, Sean's... er..."

"Girlfriend," Olivia answers for me.

Her proclamation makes my heart twist, and I can't stop staring down at her and replaying the easy way she just announced herself as mine.

Jenny holds her hand out to me and then to Olivia. "Nice to meet you."

"Sorry about all the craziness," I apologize.

Owen drapes his arm around Jenny's shoulders and pulls her against his side.

"No need," Jenny scoffs, letting her head rest against my brother's shoulder. "This kind of thing never happens around here. You just gave everyone enough tea to keep their cups filled for the next year."

"Hey, Sean, sorry to interrupt," the officer who tased Darren says as he ambles over to our group. "I need to get some statements from you, then you'll be free to go."

Owen steps back, and I don't miss the way he keeps Jenny pressed into his side. "Come up to the house tonight for dinner," he says before turning and leaving.

I watch them for a moment, then introduce Olivia to the officer. "This is officer Sanchez," I press my lips to her temple and add quietly, "He's an elder of our tribe and knows our secret."

Sanchez is older with more silver than black in his hair. He's a little overweight but has a friendly face. Leading us past where Tony and Brian are being questioned, he pulls a chair over to a table that isn't being used. As soon as we sit down, he leans across and asks me pointedly, "She knows?"

I nod.

His thick brows shoot up into his hairline. "Do the others?"

Olivia and I both shake our heads.

"Okay." He relaxes again. "Alright, so tell me what happened. The unedited version, please."

It doesn't take long, maybe another half hour to give our statements. Both the unedited one and an *official* version. After we finish, he snaps his notebook shut and then leans across the table. His voice drops as he levels me and then Olivia with a serious look.

"We'll go through his phone and make sure to get anything incriminating," Sanchez assures us. "The elders are taking care of any video from the guys he hired and anyone recording with their phones. I don't think there will be anything you need to worry about."

I slouch down in my seat as relief leaches out of every muscle.

Until Sanchez turns to Olivia. "You said you're from Virginia. Do you plan on staying here with him?"

My breath catches when he just comes right out and asks what I've been trying to muster up the courage to. *Ha! More like you've been too chicken shit to ask.*

Olivia's eyes widen with surprise, and then she glances over at me. "Oh. I—" she looks down at where her fingers are twining together on top of the table, "Actually, I have to fly back tomorrow."

My chest tightens. Tomorrow. That soon?

"I see." Sanchez lets out a heavy sigh. "I don't have to tell you that all of this needs to stay here. Not that anyone would believe you anyway, but this is an important secret that I'm asking you to keep. Forever."

Her eyes are wide and glossy when she looks up at him. They flick to me and back to him again as she nods. "Yes, of course. I understand."

"Good." Sanchez pushes himself up with a groan, and to me, he says, "I'll get ahold of you if I need anything more, but this looks pretty cut and dried on our end."

"What will happen to Darren?" Olivia asks.

I let out a heavy sigh, not surprised that she's still worried about the asshole who tried to hurt her.

"Since you're not going to press charges—and you can still change your mind about that—we'll take him to the hospital and get him checked out by mental health. Someone will probably notify his family, and after that, he'll be released."

She nods slowly, biting down nervously on her bottom lip.

"Is there anything else either of you need?" Sanchez glances from me to Olivia. We both shake our heads. "It was nice to meet you, Olivia," then to me, "I'll be in touch." And with that, he turns with a wave and disappears into the sea of dark blue and black uniforms.

We stay seated at the table until everyone has cleared out of the room and the staff are trying to put everything back to rights before the lunch rush starts showing up. I can't stop thinking about what she said to Sanchez. About her leaving tomorrow. I knew she wasn't going to stay, but I didn't realize she was leaving so soon. My stomach churns, knowing this will be our last day together.

"Would you like to come with me to Owen's for dinner?" I ask her quietly, hoping she'll say yes but also preparing for her excuse that she needs to pack or get ready to leave. And if that's her answer, I tell myself I will handle it gracefully.

Except my heart sinks when her brow wrinkles and she keeps her eyes on her twisting fingers. "I want to, but I shouldn't. I have to leave early tomorrow to catch my plane."

"What time do you fly out?" So much for simply accepting her answer.

"Um, it's at two. But it's a long drive back to Seattle, and I have to get there early so I can get through security—"

"If I make sure you get there with plenty of time, will you come with me tonight?" I reach across the table and clasp her hands in mine, silently begging her to stay with me. Even if it's just for tonight.

Finally, she looks up at me, and her lips are curled up in a warm smile. "Then, yes, I'd love to."

It takes the last of my resolve not to jump to my feet and pump my fist in victory. Instead, I pull her to her feet and out of the restaurant.

CHAPTER TWENTY-TWO

We check out of my room and load up my little hatchback with all my gear—well, not all of it. I couldn't fit Sean and the trunk in the car, so we emptied it out and I'll have to leave it behind. I'm not sure what to do with all the camping gear I won't be able to take back with me now.

"Consider it ransom, to make sure you come back," Sean jokes, slamming the hatch shut. Only we both know he's not really kidding.

That's a problem for later, I decide, choosing instead to focus on what's ahead.

Brian and Tony have decided they've had enough of this trip, and they are heading back to Seattle tonight.

"I am so sorry for all of this," I say, giving Tony a hard hug beside the SUV.

"Don't," he tells me with a firm shake of his head. "None of this is your fault."

"That's right," Brian speaks up as he comes around from the back.

I turn away from Tony to give him a hug. "It's not your

fault, either; you couldn't have known that Darren was going to go off like that."

He makes a sound in the back of his throat. "Yeah, well, I'm seeing a lot of ignored red flags after everything went down."

Tony looks past me to where Sean is standing by my little car. "You sure you're alright with him?" Once again, he's acting like the older brother I always wanted, and I can't help enjoying his protectiveness a little bit.

"Yeah, I'm sure," I answer honestly. "In fact," looking over at him, I can't help the smile that warms my face and heart when he waves at me, "I'm kind of wondering if he might be the best thing that came out of this week."

Brian, the eternal bachelor, walks off shaking his head, but Tony nods at me. "That's how I felt when I met my girl. Like, she was the best thing that ever happened to me."

I wrap him in another crushing hug, "I mean it, we need to clear a week so I can finally meet Carmen!"

He promises to set aside some time as soon as he gets back home, and things settle down again. I make my way back over to Sean and lean against his solid warmth, and we both wave goodbye as they pull out of the parking lot.

"Ready to go?" Sean asks me as he reaches for the driver's side door.

"Yeah." Suddenly I can't wait to leave this place and get back into the mountains where everything seems so much simpler. Tomorrow will come whether I want it to or not, but until then, I plan on enjoying the time I have with Sean.

He holds the door open for me, and I slide behind the wheel.

I PULL up beside Owen's truck and stretch my arms over my head. It's a beautiful drive, but so long and mostly over rough roads that have my back twinging. Owen appears in the doorway of his house and gives us a wave. A moment later, Jenny appears beside him with a wide smile.

"So, is Jenny the girl Owen's been *stringing along*?" I ask, quoting what Clive said yesterday. I was more than a little surprised when he showed up at the lodge with the pretty dark-haired woman covered in tattoos.

"Yup. Jenny runs the general store in town, and Owen's been flirting with her since she arrived several years ago."

"Huh." I can't hold back my grin as I wonder what their story is.

Pushing his door open, Sean unfolds his large frame from the compact car. Even with the seat pushed all the way back, his knees have been resting against the glovebox for the whole trip. As I follow him up the steps, my stomach growls loudly, and my mouth waters at the smell of grilling meat wafting from somewhere nearby.

Jenny grabs my arm to pull me through the narrow kitchen door, while Sean leaves me to follow his brother out the back door to tend to the grill. I barely take one step inside when my feet come to a full stop.

"Whoa!" There is food everywhere. Strewn across every available surface are containers of potato salad, beans, and bags of chips. There are burger fixings, condiments and anything else you might want at a BBQ.

"You showed up just in time." Jenny laughs as she passes me a beer from the fridge. "Owen's probably pulling the steaks right now, and the burgers and dogs have been ready for a bit."

"How many people are you expecting?" I ask, looking over all the food, because this is way too much for just four people.

She gives me a *oh, honey* head tilt. "You haven't seen how much these guys can eat, have you?" Then she drops her voice. "It takes a tremendous amount of energy to do what they can do."

It makes sense. Supernatural monsters would obviously have supernatural appetites. What really surprises me is that Jenny knows Owen and Sean's secret. And then I do a mental facepalm, because of course she'd know—which makes me want to know even more about their story.

I open my mouth to ask her, but just then Owen pushes his way through the door with Sean right behind him. Both of them are carrying platters absolutely laden with steaks, patties, brats, and dogs. Jenny scrambles to find a spot for the food and then hands out plates.

True to her word, the guys take care of a good portion of the food, loading up their plates like it might be their last meal.

"Told ya." Jenny giggles at my wide-eyed look.

We take our food out to the back where several wooden Adirondack chairs are setup around an unlit firepit. Settling beside Sean, I sip my beer and then moan when I bite into the perfectly grilled burger. He looks over at me, raising an eyebrow at the obscene noise I just made.

"Can you cook as well as your brother?" I ask him teasingly.

He leans over. "I'll guess you'll have to stick around to find out."

I know he means it in jest, but I catch myself growing quiet. Because I want to stay. The more time I spend with him, with his family, the harder knowing I have to leave tomorrow is becoming. But I can't stay. I have a job. An apartment. A life on the other side of the country.

You can do your job anywhere. You would have a home here. A family.

I keep thinking about Sean's parents. His mom was an outsider, like me, and she was able to accept the unbelievable truth of his father's family. Now I can see why. If his father was half as charming as he is with me, it's no wonder she fell in love.

I watch Sean as he talks animatedly with his brother, wondering... Does he want me like that?

He turns toward me mid-laugh, catching me staring. The way his face smooths out into an easy smile makes my breath catch. Then he reaches down between us to capture my hand, bringing it up to press his soft, warm lips to my knuckles.

At that moment, I'm tempted to call up my boss and tell her I'm extending my vacation. Maybe indefinitely. Except that, even if I did, I'd still have to go back and deal with my apartment and whatever else I'd need to do before making a major cross country move. No, it's best to just go back. But I promise myself I'll revisit what it will take to return the moment I get back home.

After everyone's eaten, Sean tries to help clean up, but I've been watching the looks Jenny and Owen have been giving each other. When Sean drags his feet, I whisper into his ear how much I'd like to get him *alone*. That lights a fire under his ass, and he all but drags me back to my car.

This time he dumps me in the passenger seat and drives us the short distance down the mountain to his smaller place. As soon as we stop, he hurries around the car to help me out. At first, I can't help giggling at his chivalry. When he grabs hold of my hand, I expect him to pull me toward the house, but instead we head into the trees.

The sun has begun to set, casting the forest in long shadows. Sean seems to know where he's going as he leads me to a spot deep in the forest, where no one might accidentally find us. I open my mouth to ask why we're here, when he suddenly spins me around and presses my back up against a wide spruce.

"What are you doing?" I ask quietly.

He brings my hands up and kisses my knuckles before he pulls my arms over my head and presses them against the rough bark. "Do you remember what you told me this morning?"

"A lot happened this morning," I say cautiously.

He growls deep in his throat and his eyes crinkle at the corners when he smiles down at me. "Let me help you remember."

I can just make out the quirk of his lips in the fading light as he lets go of my pinned wrists and reaches for the bottom of his shirt. Without looking away, he pulls it up and over his head, exposing smooth golden skin covering rippling muscles. "Do you remember yet?"

My arms fall to my sides as I bite down on my bottom lip and shake my head. "Not yet."

He toes off his shoes and then goes for the front of his jeans. "How about now?" He slowly lowers the zip to expose a dark line of hair leading into the band of his boxers.

My confession from this morning comes rushing back. When I admitted to him that I wanted him to fuck me as a squatch. Did I really tell him that?

Yes. Yes, I did.

My breath starts coming faster. Is that what this is? Is this really going to happen?

"I think it's starting to come back to me," I tease, watching him push the denim, along with his boxers, down his long legs. His cock bobs between us when he kicks his pants aside and straightens to his full, gloriously nude height. My mouth goes dry, and my heart flutters madly in my chest.

"This is your last chance to say no," he warns me. "Are you sure you want me like… that?"

Do I? *Hell yeah, I do!*

I nod, then suck in a sharp breath because one moment he's human, and the next he's *not*. In his place is a towering creature covered in reddish-brown fur with an inhuman face and huge hands tipped with sharp claws.

There is no resemblance between this creature and the man who stood before me a moment earlier. Until I look into his eyes. Even in the darkness, I would recognize the melted chocolate brown orbs that watch me carefully. He doesn't move, watching me for any sign I'm going to back down.

My fingers dig into the rough bark behind me as I take in his massive frame before meeting his intense gaze. "I want you every way I can have you," I tell him honestly.

Sean lets out a deep grunt before lunging at me. I barely have time to squeak before his huge hands wrap around my waist. He lifts me up and pins my back against the tree, so my legs are stretched around his wide hips, and my feet dangle several feet off the ground.

Oh! That's not all that's between my legs either. I can feel him growing huge and thick between us.

He lets out a softer grunt and then gently strokes my hair back from my face, gazing deep into my eyes as he rolls his hips, rocking his length against me. He's so different like this, and yet the care he takes when he touches me is the same.

Reaching up between us, I cup the side of his face, surprised at how soft the long, shaggy hair is. I lean forward and gently press my lips to his, finding them soft and plush as well. And not unlike the kisses we shared when he was human.

"Is that okay?" I ask when I pull back.

He grunts his affirmation before pressing his lips to mine. Harder. His tongue flicks out to tease at the seam, asking for permission, which I gladly give him. Tilting my head, I open for him, meeting his thick, blunt tongue with eager strokes. He tastes the same. Earthy with just a hint of mint. His teeth are different though, large and blunt except for his curved canines. When I lick one, he shivers and presses himself harder between my legs, making me moan into his mouth.

"Sean, please," I pant, pulling back just enough to look into his eyes once more. "I want you."

Carefully, he sets me down so he can tug at my shirt with his huge hands. I lift my arms, and he wastes no time pulling it over my head. When he plucks at the strap of my bra, I reach behind and unhook it. A soft growl rumbles between us when I let the soft cups fall to the ground, and then I quickly step out of my pants so we're both naked—well, mostly.

Sean is covered in a dense coat of fur. My eyes land on where his hand is cupping himself. As I watch, he starts stroking. I'm mesmerized at the way his hand slides up and down until suddenly, a cock the size of my forearm extrudes from some sort of hidden pouch.

I've already seen it once before, but I'm no less shocked at the sight this time. The skin along his shaft is bright red, with a thick purple head that peeks out from the top of his foreskin, glistening with pre-cum. My mouth waters as I wonder if he tastes different in this state.

He lets out a surprised grunt when I drop to my knees in front of him. He's so thick that my fingers don't touch when I curl them around the base of his shaft and guide him to my open mouth. I just want a little taste... for science.

The moment the tip of my tongue brushes against his soft crown, he lets out a deep moan that I feel all the way to my core. Tension flickers across his face while I lick a slow circle around his head before lapping at his damp slit, humming at the familiar salty and sweet flavor that bursts across my tongue.

Parting my lips, I moan when he rocks forward to slide inside my mouth. He's much bigger in this form, and I have to stretch my jaw to manage his plump head. Dragging my tongue across the underside of him, I slowly stroke up and down his thick shaft while I manage a shallow bob with my mouth.

Cupping the back of my head with his huge hand, he sinks his thick fingers into my hair. Gently urging me to go a bit deeper. God, I want to, but he's too big. When he presses too deep and I gag, he pulls back.

Licking his salty taste from my lips, I'm not ready to quit yet. I lean in to take him again, but instead Sean slides his hand under my arms and lifts me off the ground.

"I wasn't done," I whine.

He shakes his head and curls his arms around my much smaller body, holding me against his chest. This position pins my pussy against his cock, so it curves up towards his belly.

I wrap my legs around his hips and rock against him. Coating him in my wetness as I try to wiggle enough so his thick head notches against my opening.

Oh boy, he barely fit in my mouth. How is he going to fit where I need him most?

With his hands supporting my weight, I reach between

us and wrap my fingers around his length. At my touch, he tips his head back with a moan as I slide him back and forth through my lips. I'm absolutely drenched, and I'm gonna need him nice and wet too. My breath catches when I drag him over my clit and then back down to notch at my tight opening.

"You're going to be a tight fit." I wiggle my hips a little more and he slips inside.

My breath catches as the tip of his head stretches me past anything I've ever felt before. He lets out a low growl and drops me down a little more, sinking in another inch.

"Slow," I gasp when he rocks his hips up against me, pushing even deeper. "Just... Go slow." My mind is eager to take him, but my body knows better than to rush this.

With one arm slung around his neck, I slide the fingers of my free hand between my legs so I can rub my clit. Easing the way as he rocks his hips and sinks another inch inside my tight channel.

Oh, God. The way he's stretching me, it's—not painful exactly, but it's intense.

I circle my clit some more, then slide my fingers farther back, to where he's stretching me so deliciously. Alternating gentle slides and teasing brushes, I work to loosen my tight muscles so he sinks deeper and deeper.... until he bottoms out.

CHAPTER TWENTY-THREE

My knees are shaking so bad, I don't know how much longer they'll hold us up. The feel of her wrapped so tightly around my cock is going to be my undoing.

I can't believe Olivia is letting me have her like this. I expected her to balk at the first sight of me. Instead, she stretched her jaw past the point of comfort while I slowly fed her the tip. And now I'm pushing inch after inch inside her impossibly tight pussy, and she's taking me, letting me fill her up until there is no more room for me to go.

"Oh, *God!*" she gasps when my cock twitches inside her. I've filled her to capacity, but there are several inches of me that won't fit. Still, she begs for more. "Sean, please."

And when my girl begs, I want to do anything and everything to give her what she wants. Except for this, I don't think I can give her this. Not without hurting her, and I'd never do that.

I drop to my knees, still holding her speared on my cock. She's warm and tight and feels so good, but I can tell by the way her breaths keep hitching that I'm too much for her.

Leaning down, I gently lay her on the ground and then

hook my hands under her knees, bending them up and out, spreading her so I can watch where I'm stretching her.

"Sean!" she cries out when I swipe my thumb up through her damp slit, then across the stiff little nub of her clit that she's been working with her fingers. She squirms under me, lifting her hands to cup her breasts, and pinching her stiffened nipples between her fingers. "Please, I need you!"

Moving my hands so they circle her narrow waist, I hold her still as I pull back until she's gripping my crown. Then slowly, *carefully*, I slide back in.

Olivia arches her back, and her cries echo through the quiet forest. Adding my growls to hers, I ease back out before sliding deep once more. A shudder runs through me, and I have to grit my teeth to keep from rocking into her too deep or hard.

Her back is padded by moss and pine needles as I slowly fuck her on the forest floor. Her soft keens and breathy pleas urge me on, begging me for more. Until I thrust too hard, and her eyes fly open as she stiffens under me with a yelp.

Shit! Pulling back, I close my eyes and work to calm my heavy breathing. Then I force myself to shift so I'm human again.

"I'm sorry, baby." I stretch out over her, cradling the sides of her face with my hands and covering her with my body. "Are you alright?"

Her eyes flutter as she stares at me like she doesn't recognize me. But then she smiles softly. "I'm alright. It was fine; you didn't have to change."

I shake my head and capture her lips in a hard kiss as I slip back between her legs. She's warm and wet, and we both groan as I fill her up. Then, I start a slow stroke.

"You feel so good," I moan against her lips.

"So do you."

My arms curl around her so I can hold her against me while our lips and teeth clash. Until she whimpers, "Harder, Sean. Just like that. Faster."

I butterfly her legs so I can slide even deeper.

"Sean!" she gasps when I hit that spot she loves. "Oh, right there! God, I'm close—"

I am too. The sound of my hips slapping in time with my thrusts has my balls tightening. Dropping my mouth to the side of her neck, I let out a deep moan as she digs her nails into my back. Olivia holds on to me like I'm her lifeline as her body clenches around me.

My name is a breathy gasp as she arches up and then shivers with her orgasm, and I follow after her. Holding her tighter, pumping my hips in and out before her name leaves my lips with a harsh cry, I fill her over and over again.

OLIVIA IS fast asleep in my arms, in my bed. We're wrapped tightly in my quilt, and she's drenched in my scent.

After fucking her in the forest, we barely made it back to my cabin before falling into my bed and fucking again. Slower this time, so we could savor each moment we had.

She fell asleep quickly, but I haven't slept at all because I don't want to miss a moment with her, knowing this might be the last time I ever see her again.

My chest aches at the thought and I tighten my hold on her sleeping body.

The sun slowly rises, and I watch as a shaft of morning light slowly makes its way across her pillow. It's adorable how she tries to move away from it, when it reaches her closed eyes, only for it to follow her a moment later. Eventually the bright morning light succeeds in dragging her from her sleep, and the smile she gives me is enough to break my heart. How am I supposed to live without seeing that smile every day, now that I've gotten a glimpse of it?

I lift her out of the bed and carry her into my shower, where I have her again, taking her fast and hard up against the wall. I'm rougher than I should be, but I can't stop, and she doesn't seem to want me to. It's like she needs to feel me imprinted on her skin, the same way I need to leave my mark.

After I've washed and kissed every inch of her, I make us breakfast and then feed her from my hand with her perched on my lap. I memorize each giggle and sigh she makes between bites that I alternate with kisses. In turn, she feeds me the same way.

"Give me your phone." Her head is resting under my chin.

I don't want to move, but I can't say no to her either. With one arm curled around her, keeping her in place, I drag my phone across the table so she can reach it.

"I'm going to call you every day," she says as her fingers fly across the numeric keypad, adding her information to my contacts. Then she sends herself a text, so she has my information as well. When she's finished, she relaxes against me with a soft sigh. "It'll be like I never left."

My heart twists. No doubt, she means every word and has every intention of following through with her promises. I can't stop thinking that, as soon as she gets back to her life, things will change. Long distance relationships rarely work out, right? And Olivia's world is very different from mine. Once she gets back, she'll be pulled back into the daily chaos of her corporate job. The hot week she had with

Bigfoot will quickly fade until I'm just another memory—a fond one, I hope.

We're both quiet as we clean up after breakfast. The silence stretches as we get dressed and then check the car, pulling out the gear she doesn't have room to take back with her on the plane.

"I feel bad just leaving all this with you," she huffs at the pile of her camping gear. "You can donate it or sell it, or whatever."

My stomach sours that she doesn't ask me to hang on to it for her, confirming she's not planning to come back. The truth is sharp, like a dagger sliding into my already bleeding heart.

The silence turns tense as I maneuver the narrow mountain roads that lead back to the main highway. She's pressed up against my side, as close as she can get with the console and gearshift between us. I have a stranglehold on her hand.

"You're very quiet." Her head is resting on my shoulder, but she is looking straight ahead at the thick forest-lined road.

I squeeze her fingers and bring the back of her hand to my lips. "I'm just thinking."

I feel her head nod against my shoulder. "I wish I could stay longer." When she lets out a heavy sigh, I look over at her. *Does she?*

I kiss her hand again and then drop it between us. "I wish you could too."

When we arrive at the airport, we turn in her rental, and then I walk with her to the line for security. My chest is growing tighter by the second, knowing this is as far as I can go with her, and it's too late to talk her into staying. *Why didn't I say something sooner?*

"This is it," she says softly. "I'll call you as soon as I get back home to let you know I got there safely."

I nod, not trusting my voice. It might give away how tight my throat suddenly is.

"I—I'm really glad I met you, and I need you to know this isn't goodbye for me. I don't want it to be, anyway." Her brown eyes dart back and forth as she looks up at me. Like she's memorizing my face, the way I did last night while she slept.

Another nod, as I swallow past the lump forming in my throat. "Yeah, me too." Except I can't help feeling like this is exactly that. Why would she want to leave the city where she's built her life to slum it with me in the mountains?

Realistically, as time goes on...she's going to forget, and I'll be left behind.

Her soft pink lips tip up in a sad smile. Then she lifts to her tiptoes and presses her lips against mine. It was probably supposed to be a soft little brush. A polite kiss. But as soon as she touches me, I crumble.

My arms wrap around her, and I crush her against my chest as I devour her mouth in an all-consuming kiss. A kiss that tells anyone looking our way that she's mine. A kiss to make her remember who she's leaving and to give her a reason to come back.

When I step away, we're both panting.

Her brown eyes are damp with tears. "I lo—" she catches herself, "I'll see you soon."

All I can do is nod, or else I'm afraid I'll break down in front of her and probably beg her to stay. It takes everything I have to watch her walk through security and disappear into the maze of travelers heading for their gates.

An hour after I watched her disappear, my phone chimes with a text message from her.

> LIV: I made it to my gate. Miss you already.
>

I don't respond, but I can't stop staring at it.
Another hour passes.

> LIV: We're boarding now. I'll call you as soon as I land.

I start to reply but then delete my message when it turns into me begging her to come back. I'm still trying to convince myself that this is for the best. A clean break rather than letting her into even more of my heart than I already have.

Eventually I just give up trying to decide what to say to her and make my way outside and around the terminal to where I can watch the planes land and take off.

> LIV: OMG, I just realized I left you stranded when we turned in my rental. Please tell me you thought of that and you're not answering me because you're getting a ride back home.

I didn't think of that, actually. So instead of replying to her message, I text my brother and ask him to pick me up.

LIV: We're getting ready to taxi out, I didn't get wifi for this flight, so I'll talk to you later tonight when I get home.

LIV: Why do I feel like I'm leaving my whole heart behind?

Fuck me.

SEAN: You're taking my whole heart with you...

delete delete delete...

Tears burn the backs of my eyes as I watch her plane soar up into the sky and disappear into the low clouds.

She's gone.

CHAPTER TWENTY-FOUR

It's been over a month since I left Washington, and I haven't heard so much as a peep from Sean.

My text messages go unanswered, but the asshole reads every one of them. After every message, I watch those three little dots flicker and flicker and flicker before disappearing with no reply to show for them. When I call, I go straight to voicemail, so I leave long messages detailing what I've been up to. Telling him how much I miss him. Asking him why he is being such a dick.

There have been a few drunk messages too, where I sobbed and blathered over how pissed I am at him for ghosting me.

I wish I had gotten Owen's information. I'm certain he would be more than happy to let me know where I stand, or maybe he could have knocked some sense into his brother.

In the end, I try to accept that Sean just isn't interested, and he's being too much of a pussy to come out and tell me. Even though that doesn't feel right. I've replayed every second of our time in the mountains and... I just can't believe he was playing me the whole time.

I keep thinking back to the last day I spent with him,

and I can see that he was already shutting down. A month later, I see the desperation in the way he held me and in each of his kisses. The way he fucked me—like it was going to be the last time.

But why won't he talk to me? Why can't he just come out and tell me how he feels?

Because he's a man, Liv. And men don't think it's manly to have feelings.

Except Sean never acted that way.

Okay, well, you didn't exactly tell him you planned to come back, either.

Of course I did. I told him plenty of times... *Didn't I?*

Except not once did I come right out and say the words, *I'm coming back to you.* Because I didn't know how long it might take me to get my life packed up. I didn't want to agree to a timeline that might not work out. But I had every intention of telling him as soon as I knew something.

Oh, damn. We're both assholes, aren't we?

It's late, and I'm eating a bowl of instant ramen and feeling sorry for myself—which is my new personality lately —when I get an email alert for a job match. That's become my other hobby since returning to Virginia. Searching for positions in Washington that would allow me to be closer to Sean. Most of the jobs are in the city, though, when all I want is to be in the mountains.

I'm holding my bowl in one hand as I click on the link with my other. A trail of noodles stretches from the bowl to my mouth as I scroll through the listing. It starts out like all the others, but when I get halfway down, I sit up straighter. It's a well-known company, and they are recruiting for virtual positions. Like *fully remote* virtual positions. I could be on the moon, and as long as I have reliable internet, I could do the job.

I fall back into my chair. "Reliable internet could be a problem," I mutter to myself.

Then I sit up again and start googling satellite internet and their limitations. By the time I finish, my ramen has gone cold, but I've applied for the job and set up an appointment for a quote for internet.

A WEEK LATER, I get an offer for the virtual position.

The next day, I put in my notice, and I do something I've been telling myself I won't do. I pick up my phone and open up a text window.

> ME: I've tried, but I don't think this long-distance thing is going to work for me.

> SEAN: ...

Just like always, he reads the message right away, and then the three dots appear. Over and over and over... until they stop. No reply.

CHAPTER TWENTY-FIVE

It's been three weeks and four days since my last text from Olivia.

It simply said: *I don't think this long-distance thing is going to work for me.* The last voice message she left me was a week before that. She sounded so sad, but she didn't beg me to call her back.

Shouldn't I be happy about that? I've been ignoring her since I let her go at the airport. So, I have no reason to be angry when I finally pushed her away. Except that I'm as far from happy as a person can get. I feel sick, actually.

I've tried to justify the way I ghosted her by calling it a clean break between us. So why does this still hurt like hell?

I tell myself there is no way it would have worked out. We are too far apart, and it's selfish of me to ask her to uproot her whole life. Which is a helluva assumption to put on someone I won't let argue her case.

I ache to go to her, but I'm afraid to. I've never lived anywhere else. The West Coast, these forests and mountains are all I know. I hate having to go into the city, and the area where Olivia lives is no different.

But you'd do it for her.

I've stalked the airlines and packed my shit to go to her so many times, but something always stops me. Usually that nagging little voice in the back of my head that warns me that it won't work out between us anyway. So, then I go back to telling myself we're both better off just letting whatever might have been be just that.

My phone has been silent all day. My brother hasn't even bothered to reach out to me, since he's been busy with Jenny.

Yeah, well, no wonder. You've been an asshole since she left.

I'm in my truck, heading from the ridge along the narrow road that leads back to my empty, lonely house, and I can't seem to stop rubbing my hand up and down my sternum. The ache started shortly after Olivia left, so I'm pretty sure it's not the warning sign for a heart attack, but still... I should probably get it checked out by a doctor, just in case. Except, all I want to do when I'm not working is climb into my bed and wrap myself in the sheets that still slightly smell like her.

Because I haven't washed them.

Because I'm a sick sonofabitch.

When I turn the last corner to my house, the sight of an unfamiliar van parked in front of my place pulls my thoughts away from Olivia. The logo on the side is for a popular satellite internet company, and there is a man on my roof installing a dish.

All my pent-up frustration boils up into a rage, and I throw my truck door open before I forget to put the damn thing in park.

"What the fuck are you doing?" I shout up at the installer.

"What does it look like I'm doing?" He shouts back without bothering to look up.

"I didn't authorize this!" I shout back.

"Yeah, I know. That's why she's paying us extra."

I stagger back like someone hit me in the chest. "*Who* is paying you extra?"

Before he has a chance to answer, or maybe he wasn't going to bother responding at all, the sound of tires on the rough road leading up to my house tickles my ears.

Now who is coming?

Beyond irritated that my plan to wrap myself in what's left of Olivia's scent so I can jack off to her memory is being thwarted, I wait impatiently for whoever is coming up my driveway to appear. The longer it takes, the more irritated I get, until I'm practically seething when a small, sky-blue SUV finally comes into view.

It's not a car I'm familiar with and, unlike the van, there are no company logos on it. I'm certainly not expecting anyone. It's been weeks since Owen stopped trying to talk sense into me. And the other rangers are keeping their distance from my sour attitude too.

I watch with narrowed eyes and arms tightly folded across my chest as the car pulls up beside the van. The windows are tinted just enough that I can't see who is inside, but my heart is pounding in my chest at the possibility... that just maybe...

Stop it. Why would she come back after the way you cut her off? The car turns off.

I don't think this long-distance thing is going to work for me. Her last message replays in my mind.

An eternity passes.

The door slowly opens.

I'm certain I'm hallucinating when a familiar blond head rises up. She turns slowly. Her warm brown eyes meet mine, and my knees almost buckle under their weight. She looks exactly how I remember her, down to wearing one of her silly t-shirts, this one announcing she likes coffee and maybe three people.

Without a word, she turns away from me, toward the house, and her whole face changes with her smile as she waves at the technician finishing up on my roof. "Is he giving you any trouble?" she shouts up at him.

"Naw. Nothing I can't handle."

Hot jealousy ignites in my belly that he gets her smile, and I struggle to refrain from launching myself across the driveway and pulling him down from the roof so I can throw him into his van and roll him back down the mountain.

Knowing Olivia wouldn't approve is the only thing that saves him. When she turns back to me, her expression is tight with nervousness.

"Hi," she finally says.

After weeks of not hearing her voice, that soft breathy sound is enough to send me rocking back on my heels. I have to catch myself on the side of the truck before I fall to my knees.

Maybe that's where I belong—kneeling before her in worship.

Somehow, I stay upright. "What are you doing here?" My voice comes out rough, like I've been gargling gravel for the last two months.

"I, uh, told you." Her lips tip up at the corners, and she tucks a chunk of her golden hair behind her ear. It's longer than when I last saw her. "I can't do this long-distance thing."

I'm expecting her to dress me down for the way I've acted. I deserve it and more, but instead she... *Wait*. Does she mean it? Has she really come back to me? I can't even dare to hope.

"Miss? I'm all finished," the technician interrupts as he

climbs down the ladder. "I just need to get inside to install the modem, and I'll be out of your hair."

Olivia gives me a saucy smile over her shoulder as she shuts her car door. "Do you still leave your door unlocked, or do I need to borrow your keys?"

"It's unlocked." I mutter, falling in line behind her as she leads the technician onto my porch. "What are you doing here, Olivia?"

"I told you," she tosses over her shoulder as she reaches for the doorknob to let the technician into *my* house. Before she's able to, I reach past her and brush her hand away, opening the door for her. *Like a fucking gentleman.* I push it wide enough for her to go through then step behind her, forcing the technician behind me and farther away from my woman.

When we're all gathered in the middle of my living room, Olivia steps around me and holds her hand out to the man. "Thanks so much for doing this for me. What's your name?"

"Troy." He reaches for her hand, but just before he touches her, I let out a deep growl. His head snaps to me, and he drops his hand and steps back. *Smart guy.* Olivia rolls her eyes.

"Where do you need to install that?" she asks him.

I hang back, grinding my teeth to nubs as he walks her through all the features of her new satellite internet. *That she had installed without my permission.* When he finishes, he gives her his card and instructions on how to contact him if she has any questions. Olivia follows him out onto the porch and waves after him as he heads back down the mountain. When he's out of sight, she slowly turns to face me.

"So..." she begins, leaning her hip up against the porch railing. "How have you been? You look... tired."

I'm certain there is a vein throbbing in my temple. "That's it? That's all you have to say to me? You tell me goodbye, and then three weeks later just show up like it's nothing?"

"*I* didn't tell you good-bye," she snaps back. "I told you I couldn't do the long-distance thing. Then I was busy packing up my life and driving across the country." She takes a deep breath and points one of her fingers at me. "And how does that feel, huh? It sucks to be ghosted, doesn't it?!"

Yeah. It really fucking does.

"You can't just install internet at someone's house without permission," I slap back.

"And how was I supposed to get that permission when you *wouldn't fucking talk to me?!*"

Jesus fucking Christ, her cheeks are rosy and her brown eyes bright as she argues with me. She's hot when she's riled up like this, and it takes all I have not to adjust my cock that's twitching in my pants. Or reach out and grab her, so I can pull her against my chest and bury my nose in her hair.

This is the part where you should apologize.

Except, I haven't been listening to that little voice of reason so far, so why start now? Instead, I storm back into the house in a huff, with Olivia right on my heels.

"You don't get to walk away from me this time," she shouts at my back. "I want to know what happened at the airport. One minute, you were kissing me like you didn't want to let me go, and then I don't hear a word from you for *months*. And tell me the truth—you owe me that, at the very least."

I stop and spin around without warning her, so she almost walks right into me. My hands come up, but I clench them into fists so I don't grab her. Because, if I touch her, I'm never going to let her go.

Olivia crosses her arms in front of her. "Why, Sean? What did I do to make you act like this?"

"Nothing!" I ground out. "It's me, okay? Not you."

She rolls her eyes and huffs like a fucking pre-teen. "Don't. You don't get to use that excuse."

I open my mouth when suddenly my sat phone, which I left beside my chair, starts to ring. We both lunge for it, but Olivia is faster.

"Hey, Owen!" she answers in a voice that sounds much more cheerful than she looks.

There is a long silence on the other end before I hear, "Olivia?"

"Yup, surprise!"

"I'm so glad you're here." Even across the room and through the phone I can hear the relief in my brother's voice. Then he asks cautiously, "Does he know?"

She looks up and meets my eyes. "He does."

"And?"

She lets out a long sigh.

I hear the jingle as he grabs his keys. "Don't go anywhere. I'll be right there. We need to talk."

CHAPTER TWENTY-SIX

"So, is this going to be an *intervention*-type talk?" Sean pouts from his recliner.

"It's definitely an intervention." Owen laughs. He's sitting beside me on the couch.

As soon as Owen walked through the door, I ran to him and hugged him, putting everything I've bottled up into it. I hugged him until Sean started growling, and then I hugged him even longer just because I could.

"Olivia, honey, I'm so glad you're here. I was afraid this asshole ran you off."

Sean glares at his brother.

"Well, he tried." I glance over at Sean then wink. "Luckily, I'm too stubborn to take a hint."

Owen laughs, and I don't miss the way Sean's lips press tightly together. The way he can't keep his eyes off me makes me hope he's glad I'm here too, even if he won't admit it.

"Okay, so for this to be a proper intervention, you're gonna have to tell me exactly what happened." Owen leans back and braces a heavy work boot across his knee.

"What part?" I snort.

"Start at the airport."

"You don't know?" I tilt my head so I can look over at him. I figured Sean would have told him *something*.

"Sweetheart, my brother is an idiot." His statement comes out matter-of-factly. Like he is clueing me in on one of the universe's greatest mysteries. "And when you left, he just," Owen shrugs, "shut down. He hasn't talked to anyone."

"You can quit with the *honey* and *sweetheart* bullshit," Sean grumbles to his brother. "And quit talking like I'm not right here."

"Would you like to tell your side first, then?" Owen asks.

When Sean snaps his mouth shut with a click of his teeth, I lean into the couch cushions and tell my side of everything that happened, starting with the day he dropped me off at the airport. Owen and Sean listen quietly as I pour my heart out, telling them how I texted and called but never got a response. While I talk, the sun slowly sets outside.

"Getting the silent treatment hurts the worst," I say to Sean. "It made me think maybe I imagined everything. Or maybe I read you wrong. I started to wonder if I was just a hook-up for you, and that I was acting like a desperate Tinder-ella by texting you over and over..."

"What? No!" Sean suddenly barks. "You were—*you're not a hook-up!*"

"Well, that's a relief. But it doesn't explain why you ghosted me." I wait a moment for him to give me the explanation I'm waiting for, but when Sean only grinds his teeth, I continue, "I started looking at jobs that would bring me back here. When I found one, I applied, and when I got it, I put in my notice and packed up my whole life. *For you.* To be closer *to you*. Because I felt something with you that I don't think I'll find with anyone else. And not just with you, but this place, too.

"It was a big gamble," I admit, "moving here like I did. So now I want to know *why*? Why did you push me away? Why are you still trying to push me away?"

The room goes eerily silent until Sean leans forward—toward me—with his elbows braced on his knees. He keeps his dark eyes on mine but still stays quiet.

"Did Sean tell you about our parents?" Owen asks quietly.

Reluctantly, I turn away from Sean, curious how their parents tie into our conversation. "Yes. A little," I say, Then I look back at Sean. "Your mom was...like me, and your dad was... like you. And that they died in a car accident."

Sean's eyes flick to the side, to his brother, before coming back to me.

Owen lets out a heavy sigh, "Yeah, that's the bare bones of it. Sean was sixteen, and I was twenty-one, when the accident happened. We grew up down south, along the Oregon coast. It's all small towns down there, and with the coastal range so close, it made being who we are easy. It was a good place to grow up. But life on the coast can be a hard one, especially if you're not used to it.

"Our dad met my mom when he was working out in California. They fell hard and fast for each other. When she accepted his secret, he brought her back to Oregon with him. Only, she hated it."

I don't miss the way Sean squeezes his eyes shut for a moment, like he's reliving some uncomfortable memory. Part of me wants to ask Owen to stop, because I get it. But also, I want to know more about these people who helped shape the man I've moved clear across the country to be with and who I'll never get a chance to meet.

"She tried to make it work. For him. Then for us. But by

the time Sean and I were teenagers, all the light had dimmed from her eyes. The seasonal depression had morphed into something more. The love she had for our dad, and for us, wasn't enough for her anymore. So, she left."

Owen straightens his long legs with a sigh and then leans back into the couch cushions. "My dad tried to let her go, but in the end, he couldn't handle it. So, he went after her to bring her back. We're not sure what happened then. He was gone for about a week, but we would talk to them every night. Our last conversation was positive. They'd worked something out, and our mom decided to come back home with him. The next night, we didn't get a call."

Owen lets out a long sigh. "The next day, they were both found in her car at the bottom of the seaside cliffs. The police report blamed poor road conditions and a bad squall that came through."

"Oh no." My hands fly up to my mouth to stifle my gasp. "I'm so sorry."

Sean gives me a sorrowful look that breaks my heart. I think I'm beginning to understand why he pushed me away when I left.

"Did you think I would end up hating it here and then hating you?" When he looks away, I jump to my feet and cross the room to stand in front of him. He watches me carefully, then stiffens when I climb into his lap. I expect him to push me away, but when he doesn't, I curl against his chest like a child might. "Is that why you tried to push me away? Because I meant to tell you a million times how much I love it here. When I arrived, I felt like I was coming home, which is something I've never felt in Virginia."

I watch the sides of his jaw tick as he clenches his teeth.

"I'm so sorry about your parents," I whisper. "I know

how hard it is to lose your family, but your mom isn't me. And you aren't your dad."

Sean closes his eyes and leans forward so his forehead is resting against mine. His breath puffs, warm and minty, against my lips. I circle my arms around his neck and lean into him.

I hear a rustling behind me as Owen pushes himself up from the couch, but I don't move or look over at him, even when I hear the front door open.

"If I come back down here tomorrow and see her shit still in her car, I will personally string you up and knock some sense into your thick skull with a tree branch!" he warns Sean. Then, to me, he adds softly, "Let me know if you need anything else."

I can't stop the grin that spreads across my mouth. "Thanks, Owen. I think I've got it from here."

SEAN

CHAPTER TWENTY-SEVEN

Slowly, I look up at where Olivia hasn't moved from my lap. She's still watching me. Her beautiful face is carefully expressionless.

She's still here. She hasn't left, not even after you acted like a complete tool.

"Are you hungry?" I ask her.

"I could eat," she replies quietly.

I've missed how she feels pressed against me like this. Her scent in my nose and her arms around my neck with her fingers curled in my hair. I hate to move her, but I promised her food. Carefully, I lift her off my lap and set her on her feet, then I take her hand and lead her into the kitchen—and wince at the mess.

How long as it been this bad? Maybe she won't notice?

Olivia carefully lets go of my hand and looks under the sink for a trash bag, which she starts filling with the piles accumulating around the overflowing garbage can. Yeah, she noticed.

While she's doing that, I cross the room to the fridge, only to find...nothing. Not even a carton of milk. Just a block of cheese and some half-empty condiments. I try the freezer above the fridge.

"Is frozen pizza okay?" I take the last cardboard box out and drop it on top of the oven.

"Pizza is fine," she calls back from the living room, where she's started gathering more empties that have been accumulating for the last couple months.

I preheat the oven and then start working on the mountain of dishes overflowing the sink, only to realize the dishwasher is already filled with dishes, and I can't remember if they are clean or not. *Probably not.* So, I start that, then move on to—

"Sean. Sean? *SEAN!*"

I jump when she shouts at me, spinning around to find her in the doorway.

"The oven beeped; you can put the pizza in now."

I look over to see that the pre-heat light is, in fact, off now. I toss the frozen pizza right on the rack, set the timer for twenty minutes and turn back to the dishes.

My back goes stiff when I feel her gentle touch on the back of my shoulder.

"Sean, please talk to me."

I turn around and start to look for an escape, but there is nowhere for me to go. I'm backed into a literal corner, and it's like my jaw is glued shut, so I shake my head.

She steps closer. And closer. With each inch, my heart pounds harder against my ribs. I want to grab her and pull her into my arms. But after the way I've acted, that doesn't seem like the right thing to do.

She's standing right in front of me, close but not touching, and I'm trembling all over. "Please, Sean. All I want is to understand."

Her request is beyond reasonable, and yet... I try to sidestep her. To get away.

When she reaches for me, I start to shake. The moment her hand brushes the side of my bicep, I lose control and squatch out.

Her eyes widen with surprise, but she doesn't back up or run away. Instead, her plush pink lips curl up into a smile. "Maybe I can reason with *you*."

Without the hesitation I had before, I lift her off her feet and put her against my chest. Then I bolt out the back door, carrying my woman into the night.

The warmth of summer has given way to brisk early autumn nights, but I know my body will keep her warm as I carry her deeper and deeper into the trees to the large spruce where she let me have her the last time I was like this.

Only sex isn't on my mind right now. Well, not *just* sex.

When I find myself in front of a familiar tree, I'm hit with flashbacks of pressing Olivia up against its rough bark while she let me into her soft body. I lean against the sturdy trunk and, slowly, slide down to sit against it, curling her in my lap so she's resting against me. She feels perfect in my arms like this, with her head on my shoulder and her small fingers twirling the long hairs covering my chest.

The sense of rightness is overwhelming and my squatch can't understand why I keep fighting this. Why have I been so determined to push her away when it's so easy to be with her?

One giant hand cups the back of her head, while I gently stroke my thumb back and forth across her soft hair. The other curls around her small body, holding her tightly against me. A deep purr rumbles through my chest, and she nuzzles even closer.

"Sean, I'm not leaving this time," she says quietly. "Well, unless you really want me to."

I growl, and she sighs into my chest. "Yeah, I didn't

think you did. So, I'm going to need you to listen to me for a minute, okay?"

I go back to purring for her.

"I quit my job. I broke my lease on my apartment. Sold all my furniture and packed the rest of my life into that car parked outside your house. I ordered the satellite internet to be installed because my new job lets me work remotely. Meaning, I can work from anywhere I have an internet connection."

I want to ask her why? Why would she leave everything she's known? But I can't when I'm like this, which means I have to listen. I wonder if Olivia did this on purpose. Probably. My girl is too smart for her own good.

"Do you want to know why?" she asks quietly, as if she can read my thoughts. "Because nothing was keeping me in that city, on that side of the country, except a job. I have a few friends, but no one I'm terribly close to. I haven't had a meaningful connection to anyone in so long... until I met you."

She reaches up, lightly brushing her fingertips across the side of my face, then turns my head so I'm looking down at her.

"Sean, *you* are my home. Wherever you are, that's where I want to be. You are where my happiness is, even though you ripped my heart out and made me want to clobber you with a Cast Iron pan. Being here with you is where I'm happy."

Just like before, I have no control of my shift. One moment, I'm a giant furry creature, the next I'm naked with my woman's soft body curled up against me.

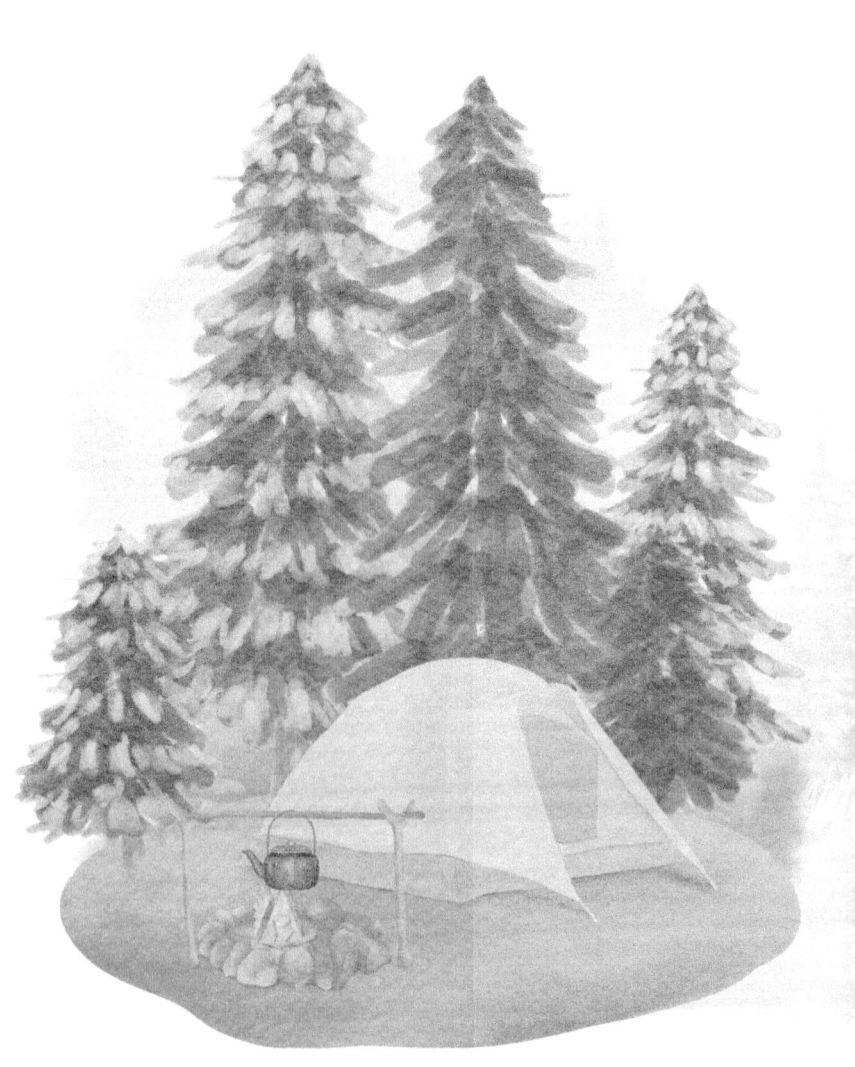

OLIVIA

CHAPTER TWENTY-EIGHT

I will never stop being fascinated with watching Sean shift from one form to another. It's an instant thing, not some painful-looking drawn-out process like in the movies. One moment he's a squatch. The next he's not. Just like that.

He's naked and trembling as he wraps his arms around me, pulling me tightly against his body. I'm not sure if it's from the cold or just... everything. I suspect it's probably a bit of both.

When I look up at him, he slams his mouth down over mine, and I'm lost to his kiss. It's familiar, just like the feel of his arms around me. Comforting. Consuming. He ignites a fire low in my belly and suddenly I need him like I need air.

Opening for him, I greedily slide my tongue against his, savoring his minty taste as I shift in his lap. Straddling his thighs, I press my aching core against his throbbing hardness.

His hands are everywhere. Down my back and then under my shirt where he slides them lightly across my skin to cup my breasts through my bra. I moan against his mouth, rolling my hips, spreading my thighs wider so he presses harder where I need it.

His hand slides up the back of my neck and into my hair, gripping my head to angle me the way he wants. And, *oh yeah,* I want more of that!

His tongue flicks across the roof of my mouth, and he suddenly freezes.

"What's wrong?" I nip at his bottom lip.

"Do you smell... Is something burning?" His brows drop low, and then both of us scramble to our feet.

"The pizza!" I gasp, grabbing his arm to pull him up.

"Shit!" But he's laughing as we run back through the trees toward his house. And I can't help laughing too.

When we burst into the kitchen, it's filled with thick smoke, and the smoke alarm is blaring loudly. I grab a dish towel and start waving it over the detector, trying to get it to stop. Sean opens the oven and jumps back when more smoke, followed by flames, rolls out at him.

"Where is your fire extinguisher?" I shout over the blaring alarm.

Sean looks around and then dives for the cabinet under the sink. I switch from fanning the smoke detector with a towel to the pizza box while he puts out the oven fire. When the alarm finally turns off, we're left in a heavy silence. Sean is naked. The kitchen is in shambles. And our dinner is decidedly ruined.

And neither of us can stop laughing.

Sean shakes his head as he closes the oven. "Are you still hungry? If we leave now, we might make it back to town before everything closes."

I shake my head. I ate my weight in snacks on the drive up here. Besides, what I really want isn't going to be on any menu. Because, my god, he is gorgeous. Tall and thick, he's cut with heavy muscles. A smattering of light hair covers his chest and legs. My tongue darts out to wet my lips as I eat up the sight of him.

"I'm only hungry for you," I say in what I hope is a sultry voice.

"Is that so?" Sean takes the pizza box from me, tossing it aside. "Then I better make sure my girl is satisfied."

My knees go wobbly, and heat floods my panties when he tosses me over his shoulder and takes me into his room—only to suddenly freeze in the doorway.

"Um, let me just change the sheets real fast."

"It can't be that bad. I don't mind," I say when he sets me back on my feet.

"No. It's... You saw the kitchen?"

I look past him at the mussed-up bed, and that's when I notice the stale scent of sex. *Oh, dear.* "Let me help."

Sean tries to argue with me, but he's learning I can be just as stubborn as him. Maybe even more.

Together, we strip the bed, and he takes the bedding straight to the laundry while I get to work on the new set. He finds a clean, if slightly musty-smelling comforter in a closet, and by the time we fall into bed, all thoughts of sex have been replaced with thoughts of sleep. I've been driving for the last four days straight, staying in cheap hotels with even cheaper mattresses along the way. So, when I sink into the pillowy softness of Sean's bed, I'm well on my way to dreamland when he climbs in beside me.

"I guess I'll take a raincheck on the reunion sex." He chuckles as he curls around my body, big spoon style.

"I just need to close my eyes for a minute," I mumble, but we both know I'm done for the night.

"Close your eyes for as long as you like. I'll be right here when you wake up."

I want to roll over so I can kiss him. Maybe push him to his back and have my wicked way with him, but instead I melt into the warmth surrounding me. For the first time in a long time, maybe since I lost my parents, I'm home again.

I WAKE WITH THE SUN, and also because my circadian clock is still three hours fast, thanks to years of living on the East Coast. Sean is still curled around me, snoring softly and lost to a deep sleep. Being trapped in the comfort of his heavy arms would normally be enough to drag me back to sleep, but then my bladder wakes up. The longer I try to ignore it, the more urgent it becomes, until I finally give up and accept that I'm not going to get any more sleep today.

I do my best not to wake Sean as I carefully slide out of his arms and over the side of his bed. The room is chilly this early, and I'm only wearing a cami and my panties. On my way to the attached bathroom, I pick one of his discarded flannels off the floor and pull it around my shoulders. Pulling the collar of his shirt to my nose, I breathe in the strong scent that is uniquely Sean, a mixture of his rain-scented shower gel and musky sweat.

The well-worn fabric is soft against my skin and warms me quickly. As I make my way to his attached bathroom, I imagine some of the heat from his body is still infused within the fibers.

When I tiptoe from the bathroom, Sean hasn't moved. His breathing is deep and even as I head for the hallway.

The kitchen looks even worse in the early morning light. The air still smells strongly of burnt pizza, and the oven is coated in a fine white powder from the fire extinguisher. Scanning the small space, I try to decide where to start first. My eyes pause on the coffee maker, and I decide that nothing is going to get done before I get some caffeine in me.

There is no milk in the fridge, so I add a couple heaping spoonfuls of sugar and then make my way out to the porch to enjoy the quiet morning. The sky is streaked with vivid pink and orange as bright sunlight filters through the trees. The brisk air smells clean and fresh, and I lean against the railing as I sip my coffee.

God, did I miss this.

The birds sing loudly all around me as squirrels and chipmunks dart up and down the trees and through the grass. Something else catches my eye through the trees, and I squint after it. I'm expecting to find a deer making its way past the house, but whatever it is disappears amongst the trees, almost as if it's hiding. Which is weird. A deer wouldn't do that. At least I don't think–

A flash of color out of the corner of my eye has me turning just as a man darts out of the trees and straight toward me.

It takes a moment for my sleep-fogged brain to catch up with what's happening, and by then, he's already hurtled the steps. I stumble back, but he's faster and grabs my arm, yanking me away from the railing.

Coffee sloshes over the side of the cup, but I barely register the burn as it hits my skin because he's clamping his hand over my mouth. Muffling my screams as he pulls me backward off the porch.

"Don't make a fucking sound!" The man's hot, fetid breath hits the side of my face, and I do the only other thing I can think of. I throw my mug at the side of the house.

I aim for the glass door, hoping the crash might be loud enough to wake Sean, but the man's arms are banded around me so tightly, it falls woefully short. Instead, the mug bounces uselessly across the porch. The damn thing doesn't even have the decency to break.

"I told you to shut the fuck up!" he grunts as I continue to scream against his sweaty palm. Kicking my legs and digging my fingernails into his arm, I scratch and twist. Doing whatever I can think of to break free of him.

We're almost to the trees, and my heart is close to pounding out of my chest as I dig my bare feet into the soft ground, trying to slow him.

Who the hell is this guy and where did he come from?

My screams turn to frantic sobs when he drags me into the woods and then keeps going until I lose sight of Sean's house. With a jarring shift, he pushes my chest against the rough bark of a red cedar, nearly knocking the wind out of me. He's hot and sweaty against my back as he leans into me. "I don't want to hurt you, Olivia. I just want your boyfriend."

I go stiff, and my head snaps over my shoulder to get a look at the man behind me. He's mostly out of my view, but there is something about his voice that makes me say, "Darren?"

He steps to the side, and I get my first good look at him.

Goddamn, I wouldn't have recognized him if he hadn't called me by name. His blond hair is shaggy and matted around his head. His face is covered in a thick, unkept beard, and going by the dirt and his stink, he hasn't had a shower or changed his clothes since I last saw him.

"I'm going to take my hand away from your mouth," he tells me quietly, like he's talking to a small child. "If you scream, I'll knock you unconscious. Do you understand?"

The way he says it so nonchalantly, I don't doubt him. So much for not wanting to hurt me, I think sourly as I remember how easily he held a knife to my throat. I force myself to nod.

Slowly, he peels his hand back, and it takes everything I have not to lick my lips. God knows where he's been or what he's touched. When he's certain I'm going to do as I'm told, he pulls a length of rope from the pocket of his filthy jacket.

"Darren, this is crazy. What are you doing?" I ask him as he pulls my arms around the trunk and ties my wrists together, securing me to the tree. "Have you been out here this whole time?"

"I need proof," he mutters as he tests the ropes to make sure I can't escape. And fuck if he didn't actually do a good job. "I need to clear my name. To prove it wasn't me who killed Johnny. I need to bring them a sasquatch."

I blink at him. My stomach twists, and bile burns the back of my throat. "It doesn't work like that. They are shifters, even if you kill one, they just return to their human form."

"Like I'm going to believe anything you say," he snaps at me and pulls the ropes even tighter, making me yelp in pain.

"It's true!" I croak. "Why do you think no one has ever found definitive proof? It's because there literally isn't any."

Darren watches me for a moment and then shakes his head. "Even if you're right, it doesn't change anything."

I bang my head against the tree in frustration. "You're making a huge mistake. Do you really want another death on your conscience?"

"I never said I was going to kill him. I only need proof that will clear my name."

I don't believe him. Whatever proof he wants, or how he plans to get it, can't be good for Sean.

Darren steps back. "You can scream all you want now. I'll be waiting."

I watch as he turns around and disappears into the

trees, and I press my forehead against the cedar again. *What am I going to do now?*

SEAN

CHAPTER TWENTY-NINE

I watch through slitted eyes as Olivia slides out of my bed.

My girl is a lot of things, but graceful isn't one of them. She's trying so hard not to wake me, she ends up nearly falling over the edge and manages to catch herself just in time. Meanwhile, I'm trying my best to pretend I'm still asleep, but I'm fighting to hide my grin.

I barely slept all night. Each time I'd drift off, I'd startle myself awake again, scared she was a dream or that I imagined she came back to me.

In the soft, early morning light, I watch her pick up one of my flannels, and my heart warms when she puts it on and brings the collar to her nose before she makes her way down the hall. A few moments later, I hear her in the kitchen, followed by the robust smell of brewing coffee.

I roll to my back and tuck an arm behind my head. I should join her, but I'm enjoying listening to her moving around the kitchen as I try to imagine what she's doing. The clink of the coffee carafe against the mug. The soft sound of the glass door opening, followed by a contented sigh before she steps outside.

Did she really mean what she said last night? About wanting to be here? I've spent my whole life watching people come and go, so I just always assumed you had to be born here to really appreciate this area. But the more I think back on the time I spent with Olivia, the more I realize she might be the exception.

I'm lying on my back listening to the sounds of the early morning bird songs, when suddenly everything goes quiet. It happens fast and feels too sudden to be a natural lull in their song. I'm already kicking the blankets away when I hear Olivia's sharp inhale. The sheets somehow wind around my feet, and the harder I struggle to get free of them, the tighter they wrap around my legs until I end up rolling over the side of the bed. I land with a grunt, and I'm finally able to free myself just in time to hear the sound of her coffee mug skittering across the deck.

With my heart up in my throat, I scramble across the room and rebound off the doorjamb before sprinting down the hallway. I don't care that I'm only wearing a pair of boxers as I skid through the kitchen then out the glass door and onto the deck. It's still eerily silent, and the only sign of Olivia is her discarded mug still spinning beside the house.

Tilting my chin up, I breathe deep to scent the air. Olivia's sweet honey and peaches scent mingles with the crisp early morning dew. But then my heart lurches, and wrinkle my nose when I also pick up on the foul scent of unwashed man and desperation.

My skin starts to itch as I step off the porch. *Not yet*, I grit as I breathe deeply, trying to keep myself calm so I don't squatch out. The trail they left through the forest is easy to follow. Just inside the tree line, I crouch down to examine the marks left by Olivia's bare feet next to a boot print.

The prints are deep and large. The tread of his boot is worn, and his stride is uneven beside the marks left by

Olivia, telling me he didn't take my girl willingly. I close my eyes and strain my ears to listen. The birds have begun to sing again, but the rest of the forest is still eerily silent. They haven't gone far.

My squatch is pushing for control. He wants to raze the forest until we find Olivia, but I hold him back. There is something familiar about the males scent. Something that tells me he is using her as bait to bring me out. There is only one person I can think of who would do such a thing. I should have followed up on Darren after he was released from custody. Made sure he left the area. But in my grief at losing Olivia, I didn't think about him once.

Glancing at the house, I consider going back for my sat phone. I should let Owen know what's going on, but that will just take more time away from finding my girl. If it is Darren, there is no telling what he might do to her. Unwanted images of him holding a knife to her throat has my squatch pushing harder to come forward, but I hold him back. Using my nose to guide me, I follow Olivia's sweet scent deeper into the woods.

I use every bit of stealth I've learned over the years as I tread carefully through the trees and bushes, until I catch sight of her. Her arms are curled around the narrow trunk of a cedar, so it looks like she's hugging it, and her wrists are tied with rope. Darren is nowhere in sight, but his stench is all around me. He's close by. Probably has eyes on her. And me.

Olivia is muttering under her breath as she presses her cheek to the flaky bark. And I have to strain my ears to catch what she's saying.

"Don't come. Don't come. Don't come," she repeats over and over. "It's a trap. Darren is waiting for you."

My smart girl knows I have good hearing, and I wonder how long she's been whispering those words. As much as I long to charge through the trees and free her, to claw through the rope holding her so I can lift her into my arms and run back to the house. I stay where I am as I come up with a plan.

"Don't, Sean. Please don't," she whispers, rocking her forehead back and forth against the tree.

Gritting my teeth, I slip back into the forest and leave her. My squatch is howling his fury as I focus on Darren's putrid scent that crisscrosses through the trees for hundreds of yards, making it difficult to tell which trail leads to where he's hiding. Is it on purpose, to make it harder to track him? I hate to give him that much credit, but when I circle a third time and come up with nothing, I have to assume he has more training than I originally thought.

I count dozens of trails and wonder how long he's been out here. Likely since he was released by the authorities. It unnerves me that he could have been watching me this whole time, and I was so distracted with feeling sorry for myself that I had no idea.

Olivia's soft gasp snaps my attention away from my self-chastising, and I'm racing back to her. My feet slide to a stop behind the prickly branches of a Douglas fir.

Darren has come out of his hiding spot and is standing behind her, with her hair fisted in his hand. He pulls her head back and hisses against the side of her face. "I told you to scream."

Olivia clamps her lips together, but she can't hold back a whimper when he gives her head a shake. There is a click, and then Darren presses the barrel of a gun to the side of her head.

"Do it! Call for him!"

My girl only squeezes her eyes shut and shakes her head.

Stupid... stubborn... amazing brave woman!

Before Darren can threaten her again, I step out into the open. "Let her go."

A sick smile spreads across his face, revealing yellowed teeth. "There you are."

"Let her go, and you can do whatever you want with me." I stare at Olivia when I say it, willing her to trust me because I know she's going to fight. And sure enough, she starts twisting against the ropes holding her to the tree.

"Sean, don't!"

Darren pulls the gun away from her head, and I relax. But then he slowly points the gun at me. "Come closer. But if you change, I'm going to shoot you."

My squatch is writhing beneath my skin as I slowly step toward him, keeping my eyes on the finger resting on the trigger. I'm faster than a human, but I don't think I'm faster than a bullet, especially this close. But maybe I can move enough to make sure a hit won't be fatal.

Olivia is cussing up a storm as she fights against the ropes. I glance between her and Darren, trying to silently tell her it'll be alright. I need her to trust me, because I'll do whatever it takes to keep her safe.

"Let her go, Darren," I repeat as I slowly close the distance between us. "If you hurt her, I won't be able to keep my squatch from coming for you, and you won't win that fight."

"Your squatch might be strong, but it's no match for a bullet," Darren scoffs as he waves the gun at me recklessly. His finger is still resting on the trigger, which is making me nervous as hell. The way he's acting, this idiot is going to shoot me without even meaning to.

"Let her go, and you and I can talk about this."

"Darren," Olivia pleads, trying to talk some sense into him. "Put the gun down before you hurt someone."

He turns to her with a snarl, "Shut up. I'm not going to–"

The second he takes his eyes off me, I make my move. My squatch rushes to the surface, and I reach him in two quick steps. Wrapping my large hairy hand around his wrist, I manage to push the gun to the side, and away from Olivia before he squeezes off a shot. The discharge is sharp and loud and makes my sensitive ears ring.

With an angry growl, I shove him into another tree and pound his hand against the trunk until the gun falls harmlessly to the ground. As soon as he's unarmed, I grab him by the front of his shirt and lift him off his feet so we're nose to nose. Then I roar directly into his face.

The sound echoes through the trees, silencing the sounds of nature. Darren blinks at me, then all the blood blanches from his face, and his eyes roll back in his head.

I let his limp, unconscious body drop to the ground at my feet, and then I use my claws to shred the ropes holding Olivia to the tree. The moment she's free, I pull her into my arms and turn to get her away from this place. I need to take her somewhere safe so I can examine her for injury. I need to get her as far away from Darren as possible.

"Sean, wait," she says quietly when I turn to run. "We can't leave him here. He'll only come after us again."

I hate it, but she's right.

Olivia pushes herself out of my arms and reaches down for the rope. "Help me hold him while I tie his arms and legs, then we should take him back to your place so we can call the police."

Again. Her reasoning is sound, but all I want is to get her away from the enemy, not bring him closer to her. Still, I can't refuse her. Putting a knee to his stomach, I hold his arms together so Olivia can wrap the rope around his wrists, much like he did to her. Next, she ties his ankles and stands up, dusting off her hands.

"That should hold him. Can you carry him back to the house?"

Of course I can. But I don't.

I scoop Olivia up and set her against my side. Darren lets out a low moan when I grab him by his tied ankles and start dragging him across the ground. Making sure to aim for every rock and root along the way.

"I can walk," she argues, although she isn't fighting me.

Her bare feet must be sore, and she weighs nothing. So, with her in one arm, and Darren being dragged behind us with the other, we make our way back to my house.

As soon as we reach the porch, Olivia slides down my side and hurries off to call Owen. I stay outside with Darren, who is beginning to wake up as I return to my human self.

When Owen arrives, I switch places with him so Olivia and I can get dressed before the police come. This time, she agrees to press charges for his kidnapping attempt, and, thanks to his insistence that I'm a bigfoot, he'll end up on a psych hold.

"I feel kind of bad," Olivia's head rests against my shoulder as we watch the police cruiser drive out of sight with Darren secured in the backseat, "since he's not really crazy."

"Oh, he's crazy." I press a kiss to the top of her head. "It just happens that his hallucinations are real. But no one sane behaves that way."

She lets out a soft sigh. "You have a point. Still, I hope they'll help him."

I nod. I hope so too.

Owen leaves shortly afterward but not before he gushes

all over Olivia. He tells her how happy he is that she came back and invites us to dinner later so we can all catch up.

Before I can open my mouth to turn him down, Olivia happily agrees, then reminds me that my kitchen is empty. "Besides, we have lots of time to spend together. Since I'm not going anywhere." She pats my chest and grins up at me in that way that I can't say no. Not that I want to.

With my arm curled around her waist, I lead her back into the house. It's hours still until we need to go to Owen's. After I close the door behind us, I reach for her hand and thread my fingers through hers before pulling her down the hallway.

"Where are you going? I was going to make us some lunch." She tugs back on my hand, but I don't relent.

"I'm out of food, remember? Besides, I'm only hungry for one thing right now, and it's not in the kitchen."

When I look back at her, her pupils are dilated, and her cheeks have turned a soft pink. "Oh yeah?"

"Yeah." I lick my lips, scoop her up into my arms, and race down the hall while she squeals with excitement. I don't plan on letting her out of my bed until I've made up for every single day I missed while she was gone.

CHAPTER THIRTY

One year later...

I just logged off from my last meeting of the day when Sean pokes his head into our bedroom. I've turned a corner of it into a temporary office space during the remodel.

The oven fire damage ended up being far more extensive than we suspected. Or at least, that was Sean's excuse for deciding we needed to update the whole kitchen. Everything snowballed from there. If we're remodeling, we might as well create an office for me, and if we're adding more rooms...

So, for the last year, we've basically been adding a whole other house onto the back of his rambler.

Working during all the construction has been a challenge, but it's almost finished now. The new appliances were scheduled to be delivered this morning, but I've been so busy, I forgot all about them. Until now.

"Are you finished?" Sean asks from the doorway.

"I am, finally." Thank God it's Friday, and I'll have the next few days to spend working on the house. Turns out, remodeling can be a lot of fun. Painting especially is turning into my new favorite hobby, which means every room in Sean's house is now a different color.

"I have a surprise for you." He's practically vibrating with pent-up excitement as he reaches out to me. This makes me nervous because, in the last year, I've discovered Sean's idea of a surprise is always over the top, so I can't begin to imagine what he's done this time.

Threading my fingers through his, I let him pull me through the house and into the kitchen, where everything is sparkling and brand-new. Including the new appliances.

"Oh!" The quartz countertop is a bright contrast to the dark mocha cupboards. A huge farmhouse sink with an apron-style front and commercial sprayer takes up the back wall with a huge gas range and matching fridge and dishwasher. The matching quartz island was my idea, and the one thing I wanted the most. It reminds me of my childhood, of my mom at the stove and my dad and me at the island while the three of us talked about our day.

"Oh yeah. They came this morning," Sean says dismissively as he drags me through the kitchen to a doorway. "That's not the surprise."

I've asked a few times what he was planning for this room, but Sean kept brushing it off. When I pushed him to tell me, he played dirty and used sex to distract me. Which worked every damn time.

He turns to grin at me as he grips the doorknob. Then, with a flourish, he pushes it open and waves for me to go inside.

I take a step and then freeze. It's... an office. *My office?*

I turn back to Sean with a confused look. "But I thought I was going to use one of the smaller rooms..."

Sean shakes his head and pushes me through the doorway. The walls are painted a soft dove gray with white accents. Two huge picture windows will ensure light streams in throughout the day. An electric sit/stand desk is against one wall, with a brand-new desktop and two massive screens sitting on top of it and a walking treadmill tucked underneath. A filing cabinet sits beside the desk, and a cozy rocking chair is tucked into the corner. The wall across from the windows is nothing but built-in bookshelves.

It's... it's beautiful. And perfect. It's like he somehow reached inside my head and pulled out my dream office. The one I never ever expected to actually have, so never told anyone about.

"How?" I ask as I spin around. Only it's not just Sean anymore. Owen and Jenny are there too. And all of them are grinning at me.

Then Sean slowly bends down. On one knee.

My head starts to spin, and he reaches out to take my hand. Steadying me. Squeezing my fingers in his.

"Olivia, this ring has been burning a hole in my pocket for months," he admits as he pulls out a small black box. "I had a whole speech prepared, but... fuck it. Will you please put me out of my misery and marry me?"

A harsh laugh bursts out of my chest as I throw myself into his arms, nearly knocking him backward.

"Um, is that a yes?" Owen asks.

My "yes" comes out muffled against Sean's shoulder.

"Don't you want to see the ring first?" Jenny sniggers. "You might change your mind."

"I don't care about the stupid ring." I lift my head. "I want to marry you yesterday!"

Sean looks up at his brother, since he and Jenny were the first to tie the knot. "How fast can we do it?"

"You'll have to wait till Monday to register at the courthouse. Then you have to wait three days, and after that, it's just a matter of finding someone to perform the ceremony."

"One week, baby," he turns back to me, "then you're all mine."

"I'm already yours." I wrap my arms tighter around his neck. "And you're mine."

"Can I please show you the ring now?"

Reluctantly, I disentangle myself from him enough that he can slide a ring onto my left hand. Then I wrap my arms around him once more. I need him close. In fact, if we didn't have company right this moment, I'd be a whole lot closer.

"Aren't you going to look at it?" he asks.

"Don't care," I mutter into his neck. "I love it."

"Olivia," he says against my temple, "you're hurting my feelings."

Looking at it will make it real, and all of this is too good of a dream to wake up from yet. But just in case it isn't a dream...

Keeping my arms wrapped around his neck, I hold my left hand up so I can see it over his shoulder.

I gasp.

Everyone laughs.

"It was my grandmother's ring," he whispers to me.

It's the most beautiful ring I've ever seen. White gold with a square-cut diamond solitaire in the center and smaller round diamonds decorating the thick filigree band. It's exactly the ring I would have picked out for myself.

"But..." I look up at Jenny, zeroing in on her emerald engagement ring that sits atop her diamond infinity band. "Shouldn't you have gotten this?"

Jenny wrinkles her nose. "Not my style. Besides, Sean asked for it first."

I lean back to stare at my soon-to-be husband. "How long have you been planning this?"

"Pretty much since I jacked off in front of you in the cave."

Behind us, Owen groans, "I did not need to know that."

Next to him, Jenny bumps her shoulder against his. "Whatever, like you've got room to talk, *stump-humper*."

Shaking my head, I decide I do not want to know what that's all about. Then I lean back so Sean and I are face-to-face. "I love you."

"I love you too."

My arms tighten around his neck and shoulders, and I press my lips to his. I was going for a sweet kiss, since we have witnesses, but sweet quickly turns to carnal and… when we break apart, we're all alone.

"Let's move this to the bedroom," I suggest.

Sean shakes his head as he slides his hands under my shirt to unfasten my bra. "Absolutely not. It's good luck to christen a new room."

I let out a soft giggle. "Well, I'm not usually superstitious, but I'm not going to be blamed for jinxing anything."

So, we christened my new office, and then the new kitchen, and all the other new rooms in our practically new house.

The End

Thank you for reading SQUATCH OUT! I hope you enjoyed it and that you'll come back for Owen and Jenny's book.

SQUATCH ME! (2026)

In the mean time, please be sure to leave a review. It doesn't have to be much, just a few sentences or even just a star rating. Also, if you loved it? Tell your friends! Most of my marketing is done through socials and word of mouth so please help me by spreading the word.

Thank you again, I appreciate each and every one of you!

Love, Deysi

ABOUT THE AUTHOR

Deysi has been penning stories since she could hold a pencil. She spends most days working as a vampire and her nights playing with the imaginary friends that live in her head. If she's not writing, or stabbing people with needles, she probably has her nose in a book.

    She enjoys loud music, sunny afternoons, and leisurely trips through social media.

Also by Deysi O'Donal

Earth's Bounty series
Anna's Bounty : Book One
Bela's Bounty : Book Two
Igid's Bounty : Book Three
Shae's Bounty : Book Four
Earth's Bounty novella's
Earth's Bounty: Novella Collection

If you want something a little darker, try my evil twin, Poppy Aster

check content warnings

Monster Gentleman's Club: Dark Paranormal Romance

DEFILED

DISCARDED

DESTINED

SHARING THEIR PRIZE

STALKING HIS MATE

TAMING HIS MATE

CHOOSING THE DEMON

<u>SPECIAL EDITION COLLECTIONS:</u>

MONSTER GENTLEMEN'S CLUB TRILOGY

MONSTER GENTLEMEN'S CLUB: VOL. ONE

Lycans After Dark series

Hunter's Moon: Book One

Made in the USA
Coppell, TX
21 February 2026